Stardust

Trevor Stubbs was born in 1948 in Northampton, England. At the age of 19 he moved to London to study theology and since then has lived in several locations across England and overseas including Papua New Guinea, Australia and South Sudan. Ordained in the Church of England in 1974, he is now officially retired, spending much of his time writing. As a child he showed little promise but in his teenage years took advantage of the opportunities that came his way. It is this that motivates him to encourage young people in the 21st century.

Anna Hewett-Rakthanee, born in 2006 enjoys a range of creative hobbies from performing in a local theatre group to producing and presenting programmes for her local radio station. She first met Trevor Stubbs through a local youth group. Her greatest passion is for digital art; while

she has previously taken commissions through social media, this is her first major project. Half English, half Thai, her work has been influenced by both European and Asian cultures. She hopes that further studies will lead to a career in animation and digital art

Stardust

An Anthology of
Short Stories and Poems

TREVOR STUBBS

Artwork by **Anna Hewett-Rakthanee**

The Listening People
15 Cleeve Grove
Keynsham,
Bristol, BS31 2HF

Email: author@trevorstubbs.co.uk
Web: https/trevorstubbs.co..uk

ISBN 978-19152880-0-4

British Library Cataloguing in Publication Data.
A catalogue record for this book is available from the British Library.

FROM THE SAME AUTHOR

Fantasy fiction for the young at heart:

The White Gates series:

The Kicking Tree
Ultimate Justice
Winds & Wonders
The Spark

The Flip! trilogy:

Flip! On the Edge
Flip! Beyond the Horizon
Flip! The Daisychain

Non fiction:

WYSIWYG Christianity
(Young people and faith in the twenty-first century)

Adventures with God
(Exploring faith and intimacy with infinite God)

This anthology is dedicated to the memory of

Wal Geng Thanypiny

a young priest who was murdered as he worked for peace
in his home district of South Sudan and the many like him
who give their lives to the service of their people.

'Look at all those stars!' exclaimed Sarah. 'They say that for every person on earth there's a hundred of them just in our Milky Way, without counting all the billions of other galaxies.'

Contents

Introduction

Welcome to *Stardust*. It is a harvest of accumulated jottings written for a variety of audiences, young and old. *Stardust* celebrates the whole creation and recognises that every human being, like everything else, is created from the elements manufactured in the heart of the stars. We are not just created from the dust of the Earth but the vast and amazing star-studded universe. We are stardust.

I have divided the stories and poems into groups – I cannot call them categories – but these are rather arbitrary and the ideas overlap and could fit into other groups just as well. That's all right; I like random. I don't care to be too organised – too much order stifles nature. If the ideas here get you thinking and growing, then they have done their job.

None of us is multitalented and I am particularly lacking in the areas of music and fine art, despite having a real interest and love of them. A compendium of this nature needs illustrating and so I have teamed up with young Anna Hewett-Rakthanee whose artistic contribution is probably the best part of this book. Enjoy her creativity.

There is a lot about young people among these pages. This is not because I'm a youngster anymore but because I am who I am and where I am because I was listened to as a young person when I was a teenager. Back then, a few people in the world were beginning to take notice of the younger generation. We spoke out, protested and marched. Previous generations of young people in Europe and America were so caught up in wars, or were the victims of a society with only a privileged few, that most didn't have the luxury. In the 1960s, we didn't immediately change things as much as we would have liked of course but we discovered a voice – a voice that set in trend many of the developments into greater social inclusion which we see in Western culture today. We got some things wrong – a lot of what we took for granted back then was still institutionally exclusive. However, we demanded to be listened to.

Listening to the insights of our young people is, and always will be, crucial and I hope I still do that. The battles for equality of opportunity irrespective of race, gender, spirituality or sexuality are still being fought across the world and now, many decades on from my own youth, my passion is to

encourage young people to speak up and speak out and then to be listened to.

I am constantly amazed at just how deeply young teenagers can get to the bottom of the matter – seeing through all the self-interest of the powerful. Who do you believe, Greta Thunberg or Vladimir Putin, Malala Yousafzai or Xi Jinping, Mya-Rose Craig (Birdgirl) or Donald Trump? The fact that I can name a few influential teenagers is a sign of progress but there are millions more that are still to be heard amidst the din of self-serving adults.

But not all adults have closed ears and hearts and there are, and always have been, older people whose wisdom needs to be heard, too. An elderly lady I once knew had a favourite saying: 'If I can pass through this world and help one or two as I go, then my life would be worthwhile.' I have never forgotten that. My hope is that I can do just that, too.

My prayer is that these pages may bring you hope and light in a world that can sometimes feel very dark. It is the light of our star, the sun, which provides the light for life on the Earth – and that life inspires us with hope and joy. All the heavier elements, the basic chemical building blocks from which life comes into being have been formed inside stars. Everything from the humble dandelion with its delicate seeds entrusted with the DNA of new growth, to the complexities of the human brain is made of stardust.

The Bible calls God 'the sun of righteousness' and promises he will 'rise with healing in his wings'. Malachi 4:2. I have found that to be true.

Trevor Stubbs, November 2021

Stardust

Roaring galaxies, radiant gases,
Swinging, singing at speeds
we cannot conceive.
Remote, distant, vast ...

Swathes of stardust beyond our sight;
dark matter, black holes, background hiss;
signals from the distant past ...

Space.
A touch above absolute zero,
vast, dense, unchanging, cold.

Cold? Perhaps.
but it leaves *me* not cold.
What a gift that I,
infinitesimally small,
can yet behold, inspect, encounter, grasp this cosmos,
this stardust,
beyond knowing and yet known,
owned,
called by name:
Castor, Pollux, Alnilam, Rigel, Bellatrix, Saiph;
Centaurus rising, Sirius setting —

Their new and old names shown.

Some say:
'Look not *up* but *in*.
Go deep, learn the inside,
Find the self,
perfect the soul.
Reach in to where the distant cosmos cannot.
Women, men, children, pets –
they are your circle, your universe.
Let them be your world.
Shut doors,
seal windows,
draw drapes.
Do not try to launch out, soar and roar,
shout into cold, vast, empty space, a place that is not yours ...'

But let me say yes to *both*.
Intimate love in infinite universe.
Yes.
Live the seasons:
Autumn harvest,
Winter wind,
Spring's zest.
Summer-tinged balm.
Touch the petal-rich golden dandelion:
Blow their downy seeds into the mellow air.
Feel the warmth, taste the riches of kitchen and kettle calm ...
Treasure the hearth;
discover the slow, the close, the here of things.

Sense scents, sights, sounds;
reach in and touch your centre:
Heartbeats, mind matters, inner flutters,
body, you ... me
In here. Yes.

Look up, fear not the beyond
studded with stars, light, life –
It is not empty. It is yours, mine, ours.
Seek the eternal;
encompass the spark
that centres the heart
in the stardust from which we were formed.

Ask me not to step where it is I that is the for-ever focus,
the beginning and the end, the purpose.
Let not self-seeking cloy, sap and destroy.
Let me fly!
Free!
Soar among stars,
Seek, see my place
in the vastness of things;
Enter the endless Love that breathes life;
for it is from here that *all* that is,
seen and unseen,
springs.

Winning Through

A New Outfit

My name is Robyn (like the bird, only with a 'y'). I want to tell you about how I was converted. I don't mean converted in a religious sense – I was already a church-goer – but converted to becoming 'me'.

You see, I grew up as a princess. I mean, as a child I had all of the princess books and dolls and clothes. I was surrounded by the best and most beautiful Disney characters. I could pretend to be any one of them. In my imagination, I could be awoken with a kiss, married to the most charming of princes, and live happily ever after, whenever I chose. When my cousins were married, I was adorned in pretty bridesmaid's dresses to walk down the aisle behind the gorgeous brides. All except once when I was asked to walk in front, which was fabulous because I was the first belle the congregation would set their eyes on. All I dreamed of was the day of my own wedding when I would be the most beautiful of them all.

But a bride needs a groom. From the age of sixteen, I studied the 'field' – boys – with care. I read the magazines that explained how to act with modest seduction; I paid particular attention to my appearance. I made sure I put on just the right amount of make-up and wore tasteful but stimulating clothes. I cultured a 'natural' casual look with all the air of it having just happened – although in truth I had agonised over it and worked on it for hours. Thus prepared, I inveigled myself into the presence of the most charming of young men. To my huge disappointment, most didn't seem to notice me at all. Except for one, that is, who seemed more intent on getting my well-planned wardrobe off of me as quickly and clumsily as he could than being impressed with it. I am happy to say that I survived that physically but it left its mental scars. Was there something fundamentally amiss with me?

After a year or so, I decided to lower my sights and look for those who weren't – and who were never going to be – princes; if I kissed a few frogs, something might just happen. Even if I turned into a frog, myself, or a Shrek-type ogre, I could still be happy so long as I got a good, solid man/frog/ogre who loved me; I had gotten beyond trying to impress other girls with the quality of my catch. It made no difference, though – I still ended with the same results. No dependable male of any description came along. I turned down the third invitation to be a maid-of-honour; I was becoming desperate.

What was I doing wrong? It occurred to me that I hadn't prayed hard enough – of course, I should do more of that. 'Lord,' I began, 'grant me a wonderful man to be my husband. I am not asking for the most handsome or dashing guy but a good steady chap who will love me. Someone who will notice me on this shelf before I get too old and dusty.'

Then, at last, there *was* someone. He was quite shy and very ordinary but I was thrilled. We dated for a few months but it never really took off and eventually it petered out. I was heartbroken. Had he been the man of my dreams? No way... but I wasn't expecting that anymore. He was a bloke, and one that would have fitted the bill but he said he wasn't sure he wanted to spend the rest of his life with me. 'Lord, am I totally gross or something?' I prayed – or rather stormed at – God, in tears.

It didn't help that my parents kept reminding me of the 'biological clock'. Mum was waiting for her grandchildren – all my cousins were bringing out their photos and posting their pics on Facebook but what could I do? I needed a man!

But then, one day, it all changed. I was on my way to church when the heavens opened. I mean it rained cats and dogs but, actually, the heavens were to open quite literally. I was soaked to the skin. My face was a mess, my hair in rats' tails and my expensive high heels were full of water. I would have turned around and gone home if an elderly couple on their way to the church in a car hadn't pulled up and offered me a lift. Before I knew it, I was at the back of the church, a dripping, sad mess.

Ladies gathered around me and whisked me off to the vestry, towels were brought, and clothes were sought amongst the leftovers from the jumble sale. Then it kind of became fun! It was like my childhood dressing up box all over again. We all laughed when one of the women kept a rather bemused clergyman at bay. He must have wondered what on earth was going on in this vestry full of giggling girls.

It was then that I caught sight of myself in a full-length mirror. I was laughing my head off in odd, ill-fitting, borrowed clothes, no make-up and hair like... well, you get the picture! And what I saw was 'me' for the first time in a very long while... and I *liked* her!

Later, as I came up for communion, I felt so good – so light and wonderful. It was...wow!– I was, like, so alive! I kind of heard God say:

'Welcome stranger. At last, you've come as the real you. I couldn't do much with the pretend one but now...!'

When I got home, I picked up a message on Facebook. It was from one of the friends for whom I had acted as a bridesmaid. It simply said, 'Robyn, my husband has left me. Says he has found someone new. Can I come and stay at yours for a few days? I need to get away. I need a friend. I need to talk to someone like you. Love Ellen x.'

'Oh, Ellen. Of course, you can!' I responded. My heart went out to her. A year ago I would have swapped with her any time – I remember feeling so jealous on her wedding day but, now I was happy being 'me', I had something to give. Oh, poor Ellen.

I decided I disagreed with Tennyson – it is *not* better to have loved and lost than never to have loved at all. Being in love is not everything, I concluded. It's *being* loved that mattered and I reflected on just how loved I had been over the years and was now.

The following day, as I was awaiting a grateful Ellen to arrive, my mother rang to say that a 'likely male' had moved in over the road. The next time I called she would introduce me. 'So do make an effort, darling,' she said. I could see her clutching at the straws – straws I somehow was quite happy, henceforth, to ignore. I had undergone a conversion!

'I'll come in my new outfit,' I declared. 'I got it at the church last Sunday.'

The Fight

'Jihad bitai', 'mein kampf', 'my struggle'.
Each to his/her fight. Immersed in life's trouble
It begins at our beginning
       as we fight for the arms of a mother encircling another
– resentment, rivalry, quarrel and hate are learned through sister and brother.

'Evil lies at *their* door – not mine,' you say.
'Evil is *out there* where my enemy stays.
Let me name it, show it, shame it, fight it,
       – *my* fight, *my* struggle, *my* crusade.
I hate those that have, while I have not.
       – let *them* bend, brake and share my pain.
Let me root out the evil of the wealthy well-to-do,
       winners wielding power and learning,
       – assets stolen from what should be mine,
       leaving me with little, depressed and lame.
Let *them* suffer, let them know strife and shame.

'Evil comes dressed as a lamb; be not deceived.
It will enter by the back door, unadorned, unperceived
Tempting, alluring, meekly making hard hearts soft.
But justice and truth for my cause will not be lost,
Let my hardened heart keep creeping evil at bay,
Enduring pure, untainted,
       untarnished by modern way;
Let me exorcise the dirt of deviance and despair
In my fight against the evil *out there*.

'Let me fight with every muscle, every weapon – arms, ether and word.
Give me guns, RPG and IED.
Let me tweet, sow seeds of destruction in computer and phone,
Collect an army of the cheated, downtrodden and unknown.
And then let them sacrifice themselves for me
          – and for their God by whatever name ...

'For surely it is God almighty who seeks out evil
          and calls me to be his priest.
He is my God, the God of my jihad and struggle,
          the God of me.
He shows up the wickedness in those I hate,
He knows; He punishes; *His* are the ways that determine their fate.
Let my children take bomb and belt and destroy
Let the wicked and wealthy die – it is in God's employ.
Lord, give me strong words, words for the fight.
The struggle against the evil I hate,
those sons of shame who have that which ought to be mine.
'Mein kampf', 'jihad bitai', 'la lutte la mienne.'

But God says, the Holy One, the Creator of all,
'Justice is mine, not yours!
I am not yours to command; I judge according to the law
          that is universe-wide.
Who called *you* to decide?
Who put *you* at the centre of all?
From where does evil spring – the evil that knows not love and light?
It is soul-deep, heart-conjured. *This* is its place of birth.

Examine your soul, your mind and heart.

Is it true that darkness dwells *out there* but not within?

Are you truly so pure, so clean of all corrupting sin?

Should I not bring light, expose the stain that scars your part,

      even as you will destruction and pain to start?

My command is to love – even those in whom evil lays.

Fight not evil with evil, death with death – abandon violent ways.'

God's weapons are not Kalashnikov, bomb, mine and RPG.

Not gunship, tank, missile, or WMD,

or even spear, arrow and sword.

Our weapons are weapons Spirit-made:

      truth, righteousness, peace, deliverance and faith in the Lord,

      prayer, faithfulness and trust in His own true word.

'I am calling you,' says the Lord, 'to seek out the weak and love.

Find and mend, heal and tend, build up, listen, care and give.

Let your struggle, your fight be here where *my* heart and passions live.

Become an ambassador for hope, for joy, for life;

When they meet *you* let them see *me*, let me shine through your eyes ...'

'Lord, I am not worthy! How can I decide–'

'My child, you are mine; I have given birth to you.

Fear not, my power is universe-wide –

It is *I* who is making you *new!*'

You have no need to fight, you are my 'bride'*.

Put all thought of struggle, strife aside,

I am the author of life; it is I who have created you.

---

* cf. John 3:29, Rev 21:2 and other biblical references in which God's people are described as the bride and Christ as the bridegroom.

True Friendship

Have you got any real friends? I mean friends you can trust and have a laugh with; friends that will stick up for you and watch your back; friends that think about you when you're not together or whatever. True friends.

Finding real friends isn't easy. Some people seem to be really popular with everyone wanting them to be friends, while others – perhaps most – feel kind of left out sometimes.

This story could be about true friends at any time of life but the characters are three children in Year 4. Two of them found a true friend and the other... well, listen to the story.

'Now,' said Miss Brown firmly, 'take out your library books and we'll have twenty minutes of silent reading.'

Louise liked reading. She enjoyed this time of quiet – especially today when she had a really good book. She didn't find it difficult to read, and she was enjoying the people in the story but Cindy, who sat opposite her on her table, did *not* like this silent reading. She didn't like quiet at all; it was dull. She liked to be entertained and reading for herself was a chore she could do without.

So she decided to amuse herself by pushing Louise's book with her pencil. Louise had rested her book on the table in front of her between her elbows – her face in her hands – and was deep into the story.

Her book moved. She glanced up, saw what Cindy was doing and gave her a cross look.

Cindy stuck out her tongue. She waited until Louise had started reading again and pushed the book once more. Now Louise was annoyed.

'Stop it!' she whispered.

'I'm not doing anything,' Cindy mouthed.

'You are, so stop it.'

Miss Brown, hearing Louise's urgent whispers, came over to their table. Cindy saw her coming and quickly looked down at her book and pretended to read. The teacher said, 'I said no talking.'

As soon as the teacher had gone, Cindy put her foot on top of Louise's under the table and pressed down hard – all the while looking at her book as if she was doing nothing.

'Just stop annoying me!' whispered Louise again.

It was too much for the teacher. Cindy had not said a word or even looked up this time but Louise had spoken twice and the whole class was now disturbed.

Louise. Out the front where I can see you!' ordered the teacher. 'Bring your book... Stand there in the corner.'

She got up slowly and walked to the corner. The eyes of every other child were on her. She couldn't put into words what she felt. It was just so horrible. It was so unfair! She hated Cindy. She wanted to tell someone what really happened but there was no one to tell. She stood in the corner trying to read her book but she was too upset to concentrate on the words.

The lesson ended but the teacher hadn't finished. Louise had to wait until everyone else had gone. As the other children walked past her, she looked at the floor so she didn't see Cindy's smirk... but she did hear her bursting into a fit of giggles in the corridor.

Miss Brown looked at Louise. She wasn't very cross but she said, 'After you have eaten your lunch, I want you to come back here and I will find some sums for you to do.'

Feeling stupid, Louise found an empty table to eat her lunch. On the next table, Cindy was triumphant, gloating at how stupid she was. A boy called Mark came and sat with her. He was a quiet lad who didn't talk much. She liked him. He didn't say anything; he just smiled at her and ate his lunch.

When she had finished eating, she smiled back and got up to return to the classroom.

As she went, Cindy laughed at her and mocked her. 'Enjoy your sums,' she called before collapsing into another fit of giggles. Louise walked away not looking to see how many eyes were on her. Mark followed.

'Where are you going?' he asked.

'I have to do detention.'

'I'm coming too.'

'You can't.'

'I can. I talked in the lesson, too.'

'No, you didn't.'

'I did. You couldn't hear me, and neither could Miss Brown because I said things in my head.'

'That's not talking.'

'Yes, it is. I said, "Miss Brown, that's not fair. You didn't see what *Cindy* did."'

Louise smiled at him. 'You saw?'

'Yeah.'

By this time, they had reached the classroom and the teacher was sitting at her desk.

'Good. Come in. I'm surprised at you Louise. I thought you liked reading... What are *you* doing here, Mark?'

'I talked instead of reading, too, Miss.'

'I didn't ask you to come.'

'No, Miss. But it isn't fair that Louise should be punished and not me.'

Miss Brown didn't argue. 'Well, you had better both do the sums then. Page twenty-one – hundreds, tens and units.'

'These are hard, Miss,' said Mark who found arithmetic even more difficult than Louise did. 'Can we do them together?'

Miss Brown was strict but she knew he was trying to be kind. Her heart softened. 'All right,' she said, ' but you are not allowed to talk about anything else.'

'No, Miss,' they both said in turn.

They smiled at each other. Life had somehow got much better.

That afternoon, Cindy was looking forward to teasing Louise some more. She was bound to be cross and upset and she would make the most of it and see if she could get her into more trouble. But, to Cindy's amazement, Louise was happy and chirpy and just ignored her – not even when she flicked water onto the picture she was painting.

Next, she tried kicking under the table but Louise had tucked her legs around the back of those of the chair and she couldn't reach her without it becoming obvious.

It didn't take Cindy long to work out that it was Mark who had made the difference. He might be a quiet boy but he understood what was going on. Perhaps other children did, too.

The last thing of the day was storytime and Miss Brown invited all the children to sit on the floor around her chair. Louise and Mark sat together away from Cindy. No one came to sit with Cindy; she felt upset and left out. That morning, she had had some cheap fun and had got someone into trouble and had had a moment of triumph but that didn't help her to have a friend.

Now she had a choice: She could either find new ways of teasing and bullying Louise and other people or she could try and be kind and helpful and, maybe, one day get people to like her, too.

So, if you were Cindy, what would you do?

Heights of Light and
Depths of Darkness in a Digital Age

A nod to the software world.

Here is the light:
Honest
Straightforward
Innocent
Clean
Straight bat
WYSIWYG
Open
User friendly
Generous
Giving
Centred in the other
Life-giving
Setting free ...
White hat hacker
- the good guy.

There is the dark:
Lies and deception
Devious
Under the surface
Insidious
Deliberately complex
Subtly complicated
Hidden
Sly
Malevolent
Stealing
Self-centred
Harbinger of death
Trapping/confining/squeezing...
Black hat hacker
- the bad guy.

The Virtual Tourist

Jason was born on a Thursday. This meant, his mother told him, that he was someone who had far to go. But Jason was also born with a congenital disorder that affected his hip. As a child, he had had more operations than he could count – without them he would never have managed to stand for long, let alone walk. Yet the doctors declared a success as Jason was able to go to school and get around the house. He could also manage to walk to the school bus on a good day – but most days his mother would drive him so he could get through to lunchtime before the pain got too bad.

Jason was one of those unusual kids who loved languages. While most of his mates mucked around in French, he persisted. From French, he moved on to German, then Italian. At church, he met a family from Sweden and he was soon into Swedish, too.

It was when he became eighteen and his mates were going off in different directions that the immensity of Jason's limitations hit home. Travelling for long was impossible – his hip would seize up and the pain would become unbearable. Taking a half-hour bus journey into town was his limit. He used to ask people about where they had gone to and what they had done on their holidays. They would tell him about Rome, Norway, America and Scotland. At his desk, he would look these places up on Google maps and zoom in on satellite-view and then browse the street-view images with the little yellow man for hours. Soon he could talk about these places and amaze his friends with in-depth knowledge as if he had actually been there.

Sometimes he set up his own journey of discovery. He would select a place at random – somewhere that sounded interesting – and then another place and follow the directions between them, tracing the route a hop at a time, stopping and dragging his mouse to look at coastal landscapes, lakesides, forests, mountains and city streets. Once he spent days travelling the route from Murmansk to Vladivostok. The pictures showed shops, houses and people. Jason could tell you what ordinary young people wore on the shores of Lake Baikal in the summer or what the old folk used to carry their shopping in Yekaterinburg. He learned the Russian alphabet so he could read the street names and the shop signs. He studied Russian on *Duo lingo* and would have been able to ask these people the way and what they liked and how many siblings they had – if he could have met them.

When Jason talked of where he had been – virtually – as if he had actually been there, his friends became worried. He was becoming somewhat weird. They could see problems looming; their friend was going places without going places, learning languages to talk to people who were mere images on a screen.

Somehow, at some time, Jason was not going to be satisfied with this and something inside him might snap. In his entire life, he had never actually travelled more than fifty miles from his home. Something had to be done about it.

Three of his friends hatched a plot. Jason knew about many mountains around the world but he had never actually seen one. He loved them – or at least pictures of them. One of his friends had just passed his driving test and owned an old banger. It was over a hundred miles to Mount Snowdon but if they took it in stages they could do it in a day, they decided. The car, the new driver and Jason would all benefit from the breaks. With the Snowdon railway, they could even get him to the top.

They put it to him. Would he be interested in it? Jason dragged his mind from the streets of Irkutsk. He had been to Snowdon – virtually. In Google maps you can climb nearly to the top by several different routes and Jason had done them all. To actually go – wow! But he couldn't do it, could he? He couldn't sit for a hundred miles, even with breaks.

Make it two days there then, they suggested. We can put up in Chester. Jason had been there, too – it might as well have been as far as Irkutsk, though.

He was scared but his desire to travel was powerful and these three friends were fit and strong; he was persuaded... and scared. A whole week was put aside.

The venture got off to a good start. After just twenty miles they pulled into a KFC for some lunch. Jason liked KFC but had never actually eaten in and this one had a view of hills behind the car park – a view completely new for Jason. His friends were having fun, too. If that had been the extent of his outing, Jason would not have felt cheated.

The car was so comfortable that Jason wasn't aware of his hip until just before they drew into Chester and, to his utter amazement, he was ushered through the oak doors of a bright hotel, the atmosphere hushed by deep-piled carpet and a soft-spoken receptionist. It looked and felt expensive but Jason's friends waved away his protests. They didn't explain that they had had to go upmarket a bit to find somewhere with a lift. If he was leaving his own bed for the first time in years, they said, he was going to have to be treated to the best, wasn't he? Of course, Jason had spent many a night away from home but it had always been in the hospital before or after a procedure and that time away didn't count as a treat. Now he was ushered into a spacious room with a large sumptuous bed.

Jason turned down the suggestion they go out for a meal. His hip had had enough for one day – even his mind. There was so much to take in. It was like being born again into a new world. Of course, he had Googled many places but actually being there was completely different. The computer used just two senses – even a large screen and surround sound was nothing compared to being immersed in an environment with the additions of taste, smell, and touch. The scent the receptionist was wearing, the gentle draught of air-conditioning, the coolness of the sleek sheets – his senses were giving Jason overload.

Caught up in the feel of Chester was so good. It's not distance so much as difference that's important in travelling, he told his parents when he rang them. Jason sank into a restful sleep.

The following morning, his powers restored, Jason was excited by the idea of Snowdon to come. He wasn't disappointed

Mount Snowdon was wreathed in cloud but the top was clear. As he struggled up the yards that separated the top station from the summit, Jason felt the same exhilaration as, perhaps, the first person on the top of Mount Everest. His friends regretted the limited view but to be above the clouds was an experience Jason was never to forget. After all, he could get the views on the internet anytime – there were literally thousands of photos – but to be there, to feel the mist on his skin and the wind in his hair, to smell the moss and the peat, to hear the clink of the loose stones under his boots and to touch the earth, the coarse grass, the rough rocks! ... The effort had been great but with all the excitement he was hardly aware of the ache in his hip.

When he got home, Jason relived his journey through Google but, as he traced the streets and paths, he could now hear, smell and feel them, too.

Now he has found other opportunities on the internet including a penfriend in Irkutsk – a girl with blonde hair and a mobility problem ... and his Russian continues to improve. Maybe Irkutsk would not be impossible after all!

Rainbows

Arcs in the Sky

Our Creator's breath! Alive and potent, compelling, comforting, sharp.
Sometimes gentle, sometimes strong but never still;
all the time, building a universe of wonders ...
The rainbow is our sign:
the whole spectrum of the colours of life
revealed where the storm meets the sunshine,
brightest when clouds are darkest.

Arcs in the sky:
vibrant and iridescent, bright yet soft,
for all creatures in time and space, rich or poor, to see, to enjoy —
beauty belonging to everyone. No one's to store away.

Rainbows are a sign of the promise of eternal life.
They have to be shared, always new, forever fresh.
A gift to stream but never download.

Patta and the Rainbow

(First published in *Winds and Wonders*, 2016)

At the end of a long day, a tired Jalli tucked three-year-old Yeka into her bed and said a prayer.

'Tell me the story about Patta and the rainbow,' begged Yeka.

'It's time for you to go to sleep, young lady,' protested Jalli with a smile.

'I know but I like the story of the rainbow... and I promise I will go to sleep straight afterwards.'

'Well, alright.' Jalli bent over her daughter and kissed her happy little face.

Once upon a time, there was a daddy whose little girl, Patta, asked him where rainbows came from. Her daddy explained that rainbows come out to play only when both the rain and the sunshine are around together. Sometimes you can see where they start, and sometimes where they end.

One day, Patta said goodbye to her mummy and her brother, who were going to take the bus to the town. She and her daddy were going to join them later in the afternoon when they had done all the shopping for her brother's new school uniform.

In the middle of the morning, it started to rain but the sun did not go away, and soon a bright new rainbow came out. It played among the clouds for a bit and then, all of a sudden, Patta saw where it started. 'Daddy, Daddy,' she called. 'Look, the rainbow is starting by the wood.'

'Come on,' said Daddy, 'let's go and climb it.'

Her daddy found coats and scarves for them both and, taking an umbrella, he led Patta up the hill to where the rainbow began. To her amazement, just at the bottom bit of the rainbow, she saw a flight of shiny violet steps that led up the arc. They were very steep at first and her daddy helped Patta take them one by one. Soon they were high enough up to look down on the valley below them and spot their house with its wet roof shining in the sunlight. Each step took them higher and the higher they went, the shallower and less frequent the steps became and soon Patta was skipping along, high in the sky looking down at the road – a tiny silver thread – that led to the town.

Patta looked up but she could see no dark grey clouds. Above her was the rainbow with all of its colours...

'What are the colours of the rainbow, Yeka?

'Red and yellow and—'

'You've missed one,'

'Erm...' Yeka smiled and began again. 'Red and *orange* and yellow and green and blue and... and-indigo-and-violet.'

'Right, only, from Patta's point of view, they were the other way up.'

'But when she looked up she didn't see violet, did she? It was white,' said Yeka, who knew the story well.

'Yes, she saw all the colours of the rainbow blend in together, and they made the most brilliant white you can ever imagine.'

'What if you climbed the top of the rainbow instead of the bottom, and then looked up? What would you see then?'

'Then you would see the face of God. You can climb the steps on the top of the rainbow only once in your life, and that's when you're on your way to heaven. But that's a different story. Patta and her daddy were underneath the rainbow... Soon they were right at the end of the stairs and there was just a small curve there that led to the top of a slide.'

'They're going to whizz down it!'

'They are indeed. The slide was long and smooth but fast. It took them right to the end of the rainbow, which was in the happy valley of the park in the town. They landed – bump, BUMP – right in the sand-pit. And that was just where they were to meet Patta's mummy and her brother.'

'But then the rainbow disappeared...'

'Yes. It stopped raining. The sun shone brightly, and began to dry up the puddles.'

'Where do rainbows go when the rain stops?'

'They're always there in the sunshine but they hide their colours until the rain comes out.'

'Without the rain, the colours get all mixed together to make white,' suggested Yeka.

'You're quite right. I can see you're going to make a good scientist one day.'

'But you can't *really* climb a rainbow like Patta. That's only a story...'

'You can't climb a rainbow with your legs but you can with your heart. There are rainbows made of God's love that you can climb, even if there is neither sun nor rain – heart rainbows that never go away.'

'I know. Daddy can't see with his eyes but he can still see the heart rainbows made of love... I like rainbows... I've seen a rainbow in the puddles before they got dried up. Why does the sun dry up the puddles?'

'Not now, little lady. It is time for you to sleep, and dream of rainbows—'

'I bet Patta's daddy made a big bump in the sandpit—'

'Goodnight, Yeka. More stories tomorrow,' said Jalli firmly, as she kissed her once more.

'Night, Mummy.'

Jalli smiled. *I wonder what adventures lie ahead for us?* She shivered. *The older I get, the more I am aware of the dangers... but then, the longer I live, the more conscious I become of the fact that I am never alone. Not ever.*

Kingdom, Power and Glory

Kingdom, Power and Glory – dangerous words in human hands.
Many are the fleeting reigns of kings who would seek to control their lands.
'Richard Of York Gave Battle In Vain' – rainbow, sign of peace,
Iridescent, alive with colour and beauty arcing through cloud-darkened sky
Commands our hearts, our attention too, that we may never cease
to turn our backs on power-seeking, and reject each crime and lie.

He who wants to rule and govern, let him listen to the rainbow maker
and live in peace – learn to live with all that lives – give and be not taker,
stealing kingdom, power and glory from gentle Gaia's delicate balance.
Let him grow in grace and selfless love to join in God's creation dance.

Red to remind us of anger, fire and blood. Red warning impending fate
To Caesar, our fallen-rainbow Richard Three, and tyrant Henry Eight.

Orange, amber and gold come next. Riches that tempt and disrupt
Family and love. Money-makers, glory-hunters, rotting, corrupt.

Yellow, the colour of sun and flower, wheat, maize and grain
taken and stolen from hungry child for man's power and gain.

Green of life-giving chlorophyll in leaf and grass in every blade.
Cut down, destroyed, cleared, exploited for rich men's trade.

Blue of dazzling sea and sky, sapphire and lapis lazuli
All claimed – tamed by rich, power-crazed human lie.

Indigo. Power-purple boast of Roman senators and kings
Today it's private yacht, skyscraper, golf course and things with wings.

Violet, once a tiny tender flower nestled in hedgerow, braving rain and snail,
Now dusty and forgotten under developers' concrete, motorway
         and high-speed rail.

Be warned you who seek Kingdom, Power or Glory,
Whether your name be Donald, Vladimir or Xi.
Or just Tom, Dick, Mary or Aunty Vi from Battersea,
Ignore at your peril the lessons to learn of history's story:
Glory-seekers are trapped, threatened by terrorist and autocracy.

To be free and alive under the joyous rainbow of hope and life
There is but One beneath whose arc we flourish, free from strife.
Filled by grace and heaven-sent peace in faith-based certainty,
His be the Kingdom, the Power, the Glory, now and in eternity.

Rainbow's End

Once in a time of great trouble, Jamie prepared to go on a journey. Jamie's dad had said they needed to find the King and get his help because that was their only hope. The King lived at the end of the rainbow. Jamie was the eldest of four children – the youngest was still a baby – so it was up to him to find the King for his family.

As soon as the next rainbow appeared in the sky, Jamie's mum packed some spare clothes and a picnic but that was all he could carry. He set off cheerfully towards the rainbow. But he hadn't gone far before he began to wonder which end of the rainbow he needed to head for. He could make a choice yet it seemed a much wiser thing to ask someone. After a while, he met another young person, Jane, with a similar backpack and soon discovered she was on the same mission. The sensible thing was to team up. They decided on the left end of the rainbow and set out together. It felt good not to be alone.

A little further on they came across two more teenagers – another girl and a boy. These were also headed to Rainbow's End yet they believed they knew which end the King's palace was – the right end.

The four of them sat down together and discussed the problem. Jamie had a choice. He could continue to go to the left end or he could go to the right with the others. None of them knew for sure which was the right way but Jane said she thought that right or wrong they should stick together because that way they could help each other. They decided to go to the right end and set off cheerfully together.

But then everything changed, the rainbow faded – they could no longer see either of its ends. Now a new question arose among them: should they stop where they were and wait for the next rainbow or carry on in hope of finding the end even if they couldn't see it?

Lost now, the four young people decided to stay where they were. But their food was running out and there was nowhere to find anymore. Eventually, Jamie stood up and said that he was going to go on – alone if necessary – because he would rather starve trying than starve sitting around. The others complained: How could they be sure they were headed in the right direction? Jamie replied that he couldn't be sure but one thing was certain and that was they'd never find Rainbow's End if they were not moving on.

Jane declared she would stick with Jamie. The other two looked at one another and, reluctantly, agreed to set off with them.

Then a remarkable thing happened. They noticed that when they were moving their food supply kept replenishing itself. When they sat still it didn't. 'We need to keep moving, then,' said Jane. And so they did.

Before long the four met others – all on the same journey. Some of the people they met had been travelling longer than they had and seemed surer of the way to go. They met some people with a map – a map book which had been put together by generations of travellers before them.

One day, Jamie began to wonder if they would ever get to Rainbow's End. Some of these people had been travelling for years and he worried about his family back home.

He talked to Jane about it. Then others began to join in the conversation. Soon they all began listening to a wise old lady who told them she had been on the journey for more years than she could remember. She pointed to the sky and there was a brilliant iridescent rainbow. 'Can you see where it ends?' she asked.

'Yes,' replied Jamie. 'It's a long way away.'

'That is where your family is, Jamie. They *are* at Rainbow's End. They have been ever since you set off and met Jane and agreed to journey together. Just as your food has never failed, so have they been helped through their troubles. The King has helped them from the moment you began to seek him.'

'So all this time I've been going the wrong way?'

The old lady smiled. 'Oh, no. You see Rainbow's End is everywhere if you begin to look for it. You found the King when you met Jane and then again in the other two when you agreed to journey together. Every time you met and joined with others you met the King.

'So there are two things I have to do to find the King,' said Jamie. 'Keep moving and join up with others.'

The old woman smiled. 'That way you meet the King every day in everyone. Why do you think your family chose a rainbow for you to follow?'

'Because it is a sign of hope.'

'Exactly. Rainbows belong to the King. They are his throne and each time you see one you know he is near you on the earth, in the sky and all around you, taking you to where you belong, helping you to become who you were created to be – each one a unique jewel of his making. Now, let's journey on, shall we? Together. Today you will meet your family once more for they, too, have joined the quest.'

Darkness to Dawn

Deep, dull, thick, heavy, dystopian-dark clouds of grey.
Stories of despair, blocking warm sun's ray.
Why is the world so empty? Why so bleak?
Why the pain? Why we humans fragile and weak?

Yet, wait. There in the murk a spark not overcome;
Love – true, unselfish – correcting creation's hum.
A love life's light, pregnant, yearning-filled –
Warm and soft, sweet-scented, all fear stilled.

But such a love – existing not for its own sake?
True heart-given love can never seek to take.
Love unmingled does not possess, cling, claw, draw, drain.
Baggage-laden love wounds, stains, gives pain.

All-giving love demands nothing in return;
Setting free, it summons not, nor echoes earn.
Love-giving delights, joy and light floods the heart
But reward-reaping wrecks, ruins, plays a darker part.
Then love's power corrupts, crumbles, dissolves, dies –
becoming one of Bob Lind's 'bright elusive butterflies' –
a fleeting illusion – a deep empty chasm, hearts unfilled;
love's light is but a flicker and all faith in it is killed.

Worse yet for those on whom this so-called love is bestowed;
Children growing knowing, not once being fooled.
So-called love that demands and commands
exploiting youth's innocence, groping, abusing hands.

Hungry, lusting monsters sucking life to fill their need
usher in the darkness, building hate, sowing bitter seed.

Thus the world's dark greys steal, stifle the joyful love dance
That God in Trinity conjures, choreographed for humans to enhance.

Deep dense clouds, black, and red mist rage-ridden, angry, mean
Rise, claim the hearts of screwed up child and messed up teen;
Forcing its victims downward – the entrance to a dread dark tunnel looms
– doubt-fraught, horror-haunted with stark, empty rooms.

Can true life-long loving ever be found on Earth?
And Heaven? Does anything lie beyond the walls of death?
More darkness? Nothing? Silence – plain no deal?
Or ... could the impossible be possible – Love forever... real?!

God-promised rainbows – wider, longer, higher, deeper than mind can conceive
Dispelling the greys, shadow-free, each heart and soul a oneness weave.
Truth or myth? Faith or fantasy? God? Reality?
If true unsullied love were real, then heaven's power on Earth we'd see.

Yes! We need not fear, for true love, heaven-cast, *is* found Earth-side;
Self-giving *agape*, indestructible, relegating hate, wounds' hurts override.
Heaven come to Earth, people God-bound, asking, knocking, healing,
Finding love light-winning – its selfless God-sent nature revealing.

There, an intellectual insight, or scientific leap, quantum-long;
Here, a musical zing flings hearts and minds in exultation-song.
There, a spirited teen laughing – declaring she is happy and 'life is good!'
Here, the gift of a new-born child or a two-year-old wallowing in mud.

Above, a rainbow radiant against the grey. Then the bejewelled, star-ruled night –
Red Betelgeuse, vast Andromeda, Venus, her clouds reflecting sunlight, bright,
And I? I embrace that planet lady, bright, bold, love-emblem, heralding the dawn;
God-made, love-filled, brim-full, wide-awake new day ... I, you, newborn.

Moving to England

'Tell me, Gareth, what possessed you to leave for England?'

'Well, a sign... from God, really; a rainbow.'

'Wow! It must have been difficult. How easy was it to get accepted and settle here?'

'It was hard. I had grown up and lived in the same small town for nearly thirty years. I will never become English but I have been welcomed and now all my children are English. They learn only English at school. I'm sorry about that; it's good to have another language – it helps you see things through different eyes.'

'Have you ever thought of going back?'

'There are times but we like our little house and we've put down roots now.'

'It was definitely the right thing to do, then?'

'Yes. As I said, it was a sign from God. On that spring day beside the river, when we saw the most wonderful rainbow with its end in Gloucestershire, I knew we had to move to the house on the other side of the Wye. Leaving Wales was sad but the new bridge means I can be at work in Chepstow within ten minutes – much quicker than when we lived at the top of the town.'

A Rainbow Glow

'Why do you do it, Sarah?' asked Lucy. 'I mean you know it isn't safe. It can't be.'

'Oh, it's not as dangerous you think. Not when you get used to it. If you keep your wits about you, you can keep out of trouble.'

Lucy wasn't convinced. Sarah at sixteen might be older than her but she didn't always have her wits about her – not with all the alcohol and the drugs about.

'Well, you won't catch *me* out in the town at midnight,' Lucy said firmly.

'Course not. You're only fourteen... but don't worry about me. I'm OK.'

Friday night came and Sarah and her 'mates' dolled themselves up and went out. It was cold and rain was in the air but wearing a coat would be naff. After all, a girl dressed to impress, not to keep warm.

Getting on the bus, they were giddy with laughter. Sarah nearly left her shoe on the pavement and the bus driver had to be patient while she retrieved it. What a hoot.

The high spirits continued as the half dozen girls spilled off the bus in the town centre.

They were soon in the company of others – including men much older than themselves, who brought glasses of beer outside the pubs. Cans and bottles also circulated. Sarah took what she was given. She didn't know what it was but it tasted smooth and sweet.

It wasn't long before the highs and other stuff appeared. Sarah had little money of her own – she didn't need it. The lads were generous.

On the other side of the road, Derek and Mandy, wearing their Street Pastors jackets, noticed the group. They recognised one of the men; he had a lengthy police record.

Derek and Mandy had volunteered after an appeal at the local Churches Together the previous year. They had never thought about becoming involved in frontline work of this kind. Their own children were now well past being teenagers, and one had a child of her own. They were lucky, they told themselves; their children had not been difficult teenagers but they had become aware that not all families we're so blessed.

The previous winter, whilst on their way home from an evening out, they had become alarmed by something they had witnessed. The newspapers and TV were not exaggerating. The town had a problem; some kids had a problem. Perhaps they could help. They knew they would need training – but that was available.

As they trained, they learned not to talk of 'problem teenagers' but teenagers with problems. This was confirmed on their first night out when they accompanied George and had to look after a girl who had been hit by a bottle. They had tried to contact the girl's parents to tell them that they were taking their daughter to A & E but they had failed to raise them. It later transpired that the girl's father was in prison, her mother in hospital recovering from a drugs overdose, and her younger sister sleeping over with a friend. The sixteen-year-old they had rescued turned out to be the family's main carer.

At this point, Derek and Mandy began to doubt they were up to this. They always did – every time they went out. But, sitting with the girl in A & E, they had realised that if they had not been there, no one else would have been there quite so quickly. As the effect of the drugs and alcohol wore off, the girl had shivered violently, and Derek had wrapped her in his own coat. They had to pay for a taxi to take her home and Derek never saw his coat again but they didn't feel taken advantage of; in her way, the girl was grateful, even if she pretended not to be, and the triage nurse remarked on their kindness. You never know, they might have saved the girl's life, even. After that, Derek and Mandy couldn't walk away from the work. They never saw the girl again; they hoped that was because she had got things together in her life – maybe.

Sarah's world that night was becoming a wild and wonderful place. *Wow*, she thought, *this is cool*, as the street lamps took on a rainbow glow and seemed to sing.

'What's in this?' she laughed as she asked her friend, Zoe. But Zoe wasn't there. She looked around for her but the people she saw were not her friends. Where had Zoe got to? The last thing she remembered was calling out for her.

Across the street, Derek and Mandy were chatting to a mixed group of kids. They knew them. They were lively but they wouldn't be out late; they were on their way home from a youth club. As they chatted, Mandy was keeping an eye on the crowd outside the pub. They didn't trust these boys. Out of the corner of her eye, she saw Sarah slump. The man with the police record caught her before she hit the floor but the girl's head flopped sideways. Mandy tugged Derek's arm. They watched as the man heaved Sarah towards the corner.

'Where's he taking her?' wondered Mandy.

'I don't know but I'm going to find out,' retorted Derek, firmly.

By the time they had crossed the road through the traffic, the man had the unconscious Sarah in his arms and was taking her up a side street.

Mandy and Derek ran after them.

'Excuse me. Where are you taking that girl?' Derek called.

'Home,' drawled the man. 'She's drunk.'

'Who are you?'

'Her brother.'

'Can you prove that?'

'What the bleeding hell's it got to do with you?'

'We're Street Pastors. We can call the police if we think a crime might be being committed.'

'So, there ain't no bleeding crime, is there?'

Sarah began to stir. Mandy took out her mobile.

'She looks in a bad way,' she said. 'Better get her to hospital. I'm calling an ambulance...'

The man knew the game was up. These people were not going to go away. He tossed the semi-conscious girl at Derek who just managed to catch her, and loped off with, 'You bleeding look after her then.'

Sarah had to spend only one night in the hospital. Mandy had managed to contact her family and was there when her distraught mother had arrived to take her home.

'Don't be hard on her,' said Mandy. 'All she is guilty of is lack of experience. She's learned a hard lesson – she keeps telling me how stupid she's been. She's a good girl.'

Sarah will be forever grateful to Mandy but she hasn't escaped unscathed. Five years on, she still shudders every time she sees a rainbow; it reminds her of the glow of the streetlamp just before she passed out – of how close she had come to having her life shattered. Tonight will be her first time on the streets as a street pastor with Mandy.

'Congratulations on completing your training,' smiled the organiser. 'Keep your wits about you!'

'Sure will,' she replied.

'No problem,' smiled Mandy. 'Girl knows what's what.'

Lockdown

Desert Island

Having given it a little thought, I have decided to entitle this part of my jottings with where I was when I wrote them: stuck at home amid a series of Covid-19 lockdowns of 2020 and 2021. Much has been written about these remarkable times and no doubt much will be written for decades to come. Unlike in the fifteen century, this plague has struck a world gifted – or afflicted, depending on your point of view – by a multiplicity of media for recording everything we think, do and feel and I thought I might as well add my contributions.

As a vicar, I came across incidents where people had been locked inside a church overnight and marvelled at the various methods they used to draw notice to their plight. Back in 2010, I was privileged to be interviewed for one of the Church Times' back page features. They sent me a list of questions, one of which was: 'If you were to find yourself unavoidably locked inside a church overnight, which personality would you most like to be locked in with?' My answer was one of the greatest English writers of her time, Jane Austen. (Incidentally, I was delighted to hear that a thirteen-year-old friend of Anna's – whose beautiful drawings illustrate this book – named Jane Austen as her favourite writer among all her prolific reading. The lady's timeless.)

In February 2020, a church youth leader challenged her group of teenagers with a similar question to get them talking about their favourite things and people. 'You find yourself washed up on a desert island,' she announced. 'Who would you most like to be washed up with?' With whom did they most want to find themselves isolated? It was a fun exercise.

The young people came up with various answers ranging from their favourite pop star to a school friend. Little did they know that one month later they were going to be in lockdown without the privilege of choosing anyone outside their immediate families to share it with – not even their grandparents. The lockdown turned their homes into a virtual desert island where they could no more meet their schoolmates than their celebrity dream guy.

And, needless to say, I did not find Jane Austen in my bubble, either. Treasured as her writings and the various movie and TV renditions are, they are still no substitute for real living people. Most of us are built to interact socially and nothing, even the best of technological connectivity, is any kind of substitute. I don't think I would survive long on a desert island. And I'm not going to apply for a trip to Mars, either. Exciting and tempting that that might be for a lover of stars like myself, I couldn't cope with being cooped up for the years it would take to get there and I would certainly miss the wonders of life-filled Earth when I arrived.

The following lockdown stories and poems are not all gloomy, though. There is always a bright side. So, let's begin with our youth worker.

Lockdown Revelation

'OK, guys,' posted Mel, the youth worker, 'sorry but the Youth Club is closed until the government lifts the ban but are you up for a virtual meeting? I mean, we can't do our physical stuff but we can still interact on an app called Zoom.'

Youth workers are by definition imaginative, adaptive and resourceful and soon Mel had a programme planned out with art, charades and 'guess-what-I've-got-in-my-lap' to baking (bring your own ingredients), origami, teddy bear basketball (instructions on request but not hard to imagine) and singing. They also discovered that distance was no object, so invitations were sent to friends and relations all over Britain and even the world.

Thus it was that Ben from Washing DC was wanting to log on at 2 p.m. his time every Monday. So Mel contacted his parents to ask for their consent. As she talked with them, she discovered a mutual interest in singing, all of which, of course, could only be done online. The amazing thing was that she found herself invited to contribute to a choir session in DC. Wow! She couldn't meet up with her local choir mates but could become part of a choir on another continent! Things were not all bad in a Covid-lockeddown-world, it seemed.

At the appointed time, Mel made contact and Ben's mom, Zoe, grabbed her tablet and retreated into her music room. As she propped up her tablet Mel could just make out a picture hanging on Zoe's wall. She didn't give it a second thought but her fiancé, Justin, happened to be passing and caught sight of it. Justin was an art student locked out of his college and he naturally took an interest in the picture that appeared on the screen.

'Hey, that's interesting,' he said. 'I think I know who painted that one.'

'Shh!' Mel warned immediately muting herself. 'What?'

'That picture. It looks like a Manet.'

'OK, clever clogs,' she laughed, sent her fiancé away, and unmuted.

'Like your pictures,' Mel said. 'Especially the Manet behind you.'

'Whos's he?'

'Manet. The guy who painted the picture behind you – the one of the man sitting down with a glass of something in his hand. Or, at least, my fiancé thinks so.'

Zoe picked up her tablet and scanned the painting.

'Yeah,' said Mel, 'that one, the one of a guy with a top hat.'

'How do you know it is by this … who did you say, Money guy?'

'Manet – M-A-N-E-T. He's a nineteenth century French impressionist. My clever clogs fiancé, Justin, here, says it looks like one of his.'

Zoe stood back and photographed it. Hanging in a huge ornate frame, it was a smallish picture of a Victorian-type man sitting with a small glass in his right hand resting on a table. He had a vacant look. The background was some kind of reddish-brown window shutter. 'Looks old,' she said. 'Husband Dan found it in Grandpop's garage after he died last year. *He* likes it …'

'While you don't,' laughed Mel. 'Hey, Justin, come and have a look at this if you're really interested.' Justin came over and stared at the screen.

'Is it signed?' he asked.

'Can't see anything,' answered Zoe, holding the camera up so that Justin could see the details for himself.

'I don't think we can see all of the painting,' suggested Justin. 'Some of it might be behind the frame.'

'Excuses!' laughed Mel. 'You're dying to prove you were right. He loves pictures; you should see his gallery of prints one day.'

'I don't think this one's a print,' observed Zoe. 'Looks like oil paint. A reproduction, I guess.'

'Can we get back to the singing?' sighed Mel. She wasn't going to let Justin high-jack her session.

As Mel and Justin were preparing for bed that night, Justin couldn't get the 'Manet' out of his mind. He lay down but sleep wouldn't come. At one o'clock in the morning, he was up looking through his art books and searching the web. And then he found it! In 1937, the Nazis were sending leading Jewish families to concentration camps and impounding their art collections. One, Jacob Meyer, had catalogued all his paintings and had lodged the list with his insurance company. On this list was a painting by Edouard Manet entitled *Le Buveur Solitaire*. It showed a man seated at a table with a glass of absinthe and a barmaid standing to his right with a carafe in hand. The top-hatted gentleman was the same man as in Dan's picture. A painting which had been lost for more than seventy years!

'If this is a copy,' he whispered to himself,' it must have been made at least seventy-four years ago, and, from what I could see on the screen, it's a pretty good one!'

The morning came. It took a long time but it came.

'OK,' said Justin. 'What are we going to do about it?'

'Do about what?' asked Mel as she sipped the tea he had brought her.

'The Manet in Washington DC.'

'Nothing. It's not our business.'

'But if that is a darn good copy, then they had better do something with their insurance. And if it is the original or part of it, it was stolen; it doesn't belong to them.'

'Look, Justin. My Zoom meetings are private. You shouldn't even have been looking!'

'I wasn't spying – I just couldn't help noticing. And if a picture of a lost masterpiece comes on the screen, what am I supposed to do?!'

'OK. I'll call up Zoe. And you'd better be prepared to get us a good international lawyer if she wants to make a fuss.'

'Seriously, though. If we *didn't* say anything then we could be guilty of some law. Imagine!'

'It's in the USA, for goodness sake, Justin! but we'll just say what we – you – think and leave it to them. Then you'll be happy and that will be the end of it.'

Justin was obviously not happy with the thought of it all fizzling out. But, after a moment during which Mel stood and waited, he relented. 'OK. I guess you're right.'

'I am right.'

Mel messaged Zoe.

Two weeks passed and Zoe emailed Mel. They had contacted the National Gallery of Art in Constitution Avenue, Washington DC and, despite the lockdown, they had dispatched an assessor wearing a face mask. He had studied the painting, taken it off the wall, examined the reverse, pointed out that indeed much of the painting was obscured by the frame, given them a receipt and taken it away.

The following day, the gallery phoned to say they had received the painting and that they had removed it from its frame to reveal a buxom barmaid! Probably deliberately excluded by someone of a prudish nature.

'Wow, Zoe!' said Mel. 'So when will you know if it's the original?'

'Lord knows... If it is, it will have taken *us* to be locked in to set *it* free! To tell you the truth, I'm glad; I've already replaced it... with a photo of our Zoom choir. I didn't like the look of the drinker; I dread to think what the barmaid looks like!'

'You're not going to get it back?'

'Original or a copy, it is better in a gallery,' laughed Zoe.

'But isn't it valuable?'

'No doubt. But it isn't ours. Its provenance is established and has to be returned but, unless we object, we can be mentioned as the temporary keepers but the credit for its discovery belongs to your Justin. Can I tell them where you live?'

A month later a letter from the National Gallery of Art arrived through Mel's letterbox addressed to Justin. He was in the bathroom. She put it on his desk where he would see it and called out that she was going to the shops. As she went, she hummed the choral piece she had been practising for the choir in Washington. It might be a lockdown world but it was a small one.

Justin came out of the shower and tore the letter open. It was a short letter.

> *Dear Mr Jones,*
>
> *At the recommendation of the current owners, George and Zoe Planter, in Washington DC, I am writing to record our appreciation of your observation regarding the hitherto lost work,* Le Buveur Solitaire, *by Edouard Manet.*
>
> *On examining the work in question, our in-house experts are of the opinion that there is a strong possibility that it is the lost masterpiece.*
>
> *As you are no doubt aware, the work was stolen by the Nazi régime in the late 1930s and it is incumbent upon us to trace the*

rightful owners. When we have done this we will discuss with them the necessary procedures needed to establish the status of the work. This will inevitably take some time, particularly in this period of lockdown and travel restrictions but in due course, it is hoped, a definitive decision might be reached.

I am sure that Mr and Mrs Planter will keep you informed of our progress. In the meantime when restrictions allow and given due notice if you wanted to visit the gallery to examine the painting yourself, you are most welcome to do so.

Kind regards,
Miranda Clarke
Associate Curator

When Mel got back home, Justine was still not dressed. He was on his computer trying to work out how much it would cost to get to Washington DC and was exhibiting frustration that the airlines were giving him little hope of the lockdown letting up any time soon.

Mel put her arms around him from behind and whispered into her man's ear. 'The lockdown gives and the lockdown takes away. The life of an expert commands patience, it seems. In the meantime, shall I ask all my friends to examine their lofts to find any lost masterpieces for you to appraise?'

But Justin said nothing. He wasn't listening.

Half an hour later, Justin was still engaged in his computer research. Mel put a mug of tea beside him. He reached out a hand and put it to his lips without saying a word. His gaze on the screen reminded her of the gaze of *Le Buveur Solitaire*: 'The Solitary Drinker'.

Mel smiled to herself. *Perhaps if I were to dress like a nineteenth-century Parisian barmaid, that might just get his attention... or perhaps a tot of absinthe in his tea might be the more effective option!*

Locked Down Town

Shut in, shut out! How dare they? How can we be shut down?!
The shock! The eerie stillness, empty streets, shops shuttered, locked down town ...

How can it be us? We're never in line for anything vile.
Nine-eleven, Boxing Day two thousand and four,
Hurricane Katrina, Ukraine, Japan but never on our shores.
The UK is immune, the wars, the unspeakable laws –
always abroad, over there, never on our exclusive isle.

The hospitals are full. Silent church bells stand, unrung.
'Never like this in the war!' declares an elderly woman denied
a visit from her nearest and dearest. Not even at her bedside
as life slips away. No one but an unknown to hear her cries –
a devoted overworked care worker, underpaid and unsung.

All is hushed with a silence of ancient times when hiss of piston,
clank of wheel and ring of steel fall still, and nature in full fling
rejoices, exults, springs into life. Listen! There in the air a feathered wing;
no screech of jet above or roar of four by four – hear the skylark sing!
Frenzy and noise have ceased and the haze of diesel fumes abate. Listen!

Hearts go out to the young, yearning to be free and fly in the passions of youth.
Longing to escape, burst the bubbles of constraint, meet up, laugh and run.
Zooming your beau at the end of the town is not like a tender kiss under the sun.
Even exams must be preferred to careless coursework, assessed or undone.
Each teenage year lost – a not-to-be-repeated step on the stairway of growth and
truth.

Church, mosque and synagogue closed to worship, fellowship and rites of passage.
Yet God is not to be found only in majesty in high heaven, remote
but lives on Earth in every heart and bubble, loving. God does not gloat
at sinful humanity reaping the rewards of wrongs repeated. Nor does God note
to punish — as a doting father, loving mother, he suffers amidst the rubbish.

It's true! Shut in, shut out, we have the rules, we are shut down.
Yet within the stillness, God lives with us in our locked down town.

Silent Signs

The following story was written for a child looking for an adventure in lockdown isolation.

Lucy sighed. She missed school so much. Children all over the city – all over Britain – the whole world! – were off school because of the coronavirus lockdown but for Lucy, it was worse. It was especially hard because she was deaf and an only child. She lived in a small flat on the second floor with her mother and no one else.

Lucy went to a special school where there were other deaf children and where she regularly met with members of the Deaf community. Homeschooling via video link was not an option for Lucy; they couldn't afford a computer. At school, she would chat along happily using sign language. She was commended for her ability to sign and had advanced beyond what many children of nine years old had done. 'Articulate' is what her teacher had called her. She was also a great reader and loved stories and that is where the library came in. She had been there every other day. Once she had even met an author who signed a book for her to keep. One day she would like to write books herself, she told him. He wished her luck and urged her to work hard. She would.

But now, suddenly, there was no school, no library outings and hardly any going out at all. Her mum had to give up her job because she couldn't leave Lucy – not that the job would have lasted – and now money was even tighter. They got out every other day for a walk around the block keeping two metres away from anyone they met and that was supposed to include dogs, too; they mustn't be patted and fondled. Lucy loved dogs and dogs loved her – dogs didn't expect conversation. Lucy missed them but there was no way they could have a dog in their tiny flat even if they could afford one, which they couldn't.

Those were the bad things. Now for the good things. These began at the end of the second week of lockdown. Lucy's flat had a balcony from which you could just see a hill with a wood on it between the blocks opposite. It was too far away to make out individual trees and Lucy watched it as it went from brown to green. Spring was changing its colour. And once when the sky was heavy with storm clouds she saw a rainbow – iridescent against the dark grey – which seemed to end right in the wood. When Lucy looked at that hill she didn't feel so trapped in. She and her mum were feeling really cooped up and she had already read her latest library book four times and now she had run out of anything new to read. The television only helped so far – especially if you can't hear and the subtitles didn't always work. And, in any case, the stuff for nine-year-olds was limited. She filled in her colouring book and then set about decorating the borders, too.

One day when she was looking at the hill and thinking about how she would run and explore there when she was allowed out again, she saw someone on one of the balconies opposite. It was a young girl; she was waving. Was she waving at her? Lucy waved and the girl waved back. Her mother sometimes complained about the din that came up from the square of tower blocks but Lucy had been deaf from birth and she had no idea of what a din was – other than it was something her mother didn't like. She was near enough to see the other girl's lips move and knew she was calling to her but she was too far away to lip read.

Lucy did what she always did when people spoke to her that didn't know her: she signed that she was deaf. The girl responded immediately by pointing to her and repeating the sign for 'deaf' – two fingers to her right ear. Lucy replied by raising her right hand and knocking the air, the sign for 'yes'. She then pointed at the girl and asked if she were deaf. The girl signed a no but then continued to explain that her sister was deaf, so she knew sign language. Lucy was now in her element. She asked if her sister was there but she explained she wasn't; her older sister was in Australia. They were from Australia but they had been visiting her grandma when the lockdown happened and now they couldn't get home.

Lucy knew that Australia was one of the foreign countries where sign language is related to British Sign Language. There aren't many. American Sign Language, for example, is entirely different. The girls spent several minutes signing and Lucy learned the girl opposite was called Paula and like her, she was nine, too. Then Paula's dad called her inside and she signed that she had to go. Lucy waved goodbye. Apart from her mum, Paula was the first person she had spoken to in two weeks. It felt good.

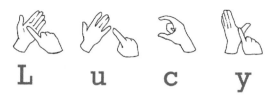

L u c y

Two more weeks passed and Lucy and Paula talked about what it was like in her home city of Melbourne and what Paula was missing. Lucy found a map of the world in one of her books and was pleased to find Melbourne marked on it. She soon found out what Paula's house was like, too. It wasn't a bit like Lucy's flat but stood on its own in a large garden with a swimming pool. They talked about their schools and all the things they liked best and what they could do when they got to go out again. Paula said they used to go to a big church called Saint Paul's, like her, in the centre of the city and that the river was called the Yarra. The woods around the river were her favourite place. She told Lucy to put Yarra River into her computer so she could see pictures of them. Lucy shook her head and explained that they did not own a computer.

'I don't know what you find to do on the balcony so often,' Lucy's mum said one day. She didn't care for the balcony. All you could see were other people watering flowers in pots she didn't have and hanging out clothes that looked nicer than her own. It was far too noisy, too. She didn't even want to join in the hand-clapping on a Thursday evening. It wasn't that she wasn't grateful to the NHS but didn't really get on with her neighbours. She'd never wanted to live where she did – it had been a case of needs must.

Lucy explained what she was doing and signed that she had a friend called Paula. Her mother shrugged. Little girls were noted for having imaginary friends; she had had one when she was a child. Lucy told her about Australia and her mother admired her for her imagination. She regretted not being able to get her daughter some new books from the library.

But then something serious happened. In the middle of the third week, Paula appeared on the balcony and began signing urgently. Lucy quickly picked up that Paula's father was out and her grandmother had collapsed. Paula said the old lady couldn't breathe. Her father had taken his phone with him and she couldn't get grandma's to work. Lucy told her to wait and went to fetch her mother. Her mother was amazed to see a real little girl on the balcony opposite. Lucy explained to her mother about Paula's grandma, so they quickly dialled 999 and Lucy's mum went out to meet the ambulance.

Lucy watched from the balcony as an ambulance drove in and saw her mum showing the paramedics the way up to Paula's grandma's flat. After a while, they re-emerged with Paula's grandma on a stretcher followed by Paula.

Paula was left with Lucy's mum as the ambulance drove off with blue flashing lights. Lucy waved. Her mum was confused about what to do. She couldn't leave Paula but she didn't want to get close either – what if her grandma had the virus? But there was nothing for it, despite the lockdown they had to take Paula in because she didn't expect her dad for hours. Lucy's mum signed to her daughter to get a pen and a piece of paper and bring them down to her. She wrote a message on the paper and told Paula to take it back to her grandma's flat and leave it where her dad would find it. Then to come back with them and they would look after her; they would have to risk the virus. Paula didn't look poorly, just upset and frightened.

As soon as they were all inside the flat they washed their hands thoroughly. Lucy said the Jack and Jill nursery rhyme in her head as she had been taught at school but her mum made Paula take all her clothes off to wash and then take a shower. While Lucy helped Paula to choose some of her own clean clothes, her mother put Paula's in the washing machine on the hot wash. Lucy showed her new friend her books and toys and soon Paula was a little happier. She had been quite frightened and lonely. They had eventually managed to contact her dad and he went straight round to the hospital.

Later that day, Paula's dad phoned. He asked if Paula could stay with Lucy – he was staying at the hospital.

A few hours later, he called to say that grandma was all right. She hadn't got the virus but had had a heart attack and was expected to make a good recovery because they had got her into hospital straight away. If Lucy hadn't acted as quickly as she did, Paula's grandma could have died. He was enormously grateful to Lucy and her mum, he said. He had not been allowed to see grandma but had been able to talk to her on the phone.

When her dad got back, lockdown meant that Paula had to go back inside her grandma's flat, of course, and, like Lucy, stay in. They continued to sign from balcony to balcony and Lucy reported to her mum that Paula's grandma was getting better.

About a week later, two big parcels arrived for Lucy and her mum. They contained a computer and a router. Where had they come from? Paula's dad of course. When Lucy told Paula about the parcels, her dad came onto the balcony and explained that the gift was a small thing for an enormous good deed. Paula signed that her dad would pay for an Internet connection for them, so Lucy would be able to join her school friends and do lessons online.

Soon Lucy was using the new computer to do all sorts of exciting things. One of the best things was that she found she could get e-books from the library. You just borrowed them like a paper book and they appeared on your computer as if by magic and then at the end of the loan period just disappeared again!

Of course, it also meant that Lucy could explore the Yarra River from the Royal Botanical Gardens to the Yarra Ranges National Park. And also, a bit about the wood on the hill she could see between the blocks of flats, too. She and Paula could send messages any time online, which meant that when the day came for her to go home to Australia they could stay friends.

Now Lucy waves to Paula's grandma every morning and, one day when lockdown is over, she will become a new friend, too, because Paula is teaching her to sign.

A February Walk

Hear the blackbird's song, crisp and clear

telling us, surely, that spring draws near.

And there, high in the air over the flat seed-drilled field

      a lark.

Hear it trill, watch it swoop, marking the season's change,

calling for – no commanding – the spring to begin and winter yield.

Here, despite chill wind and frost-covered ditch, the lane's alive:

beneath thin ice, living water trickles down a steep tarmacked track.

Each boot step crunches and cracks

releasing a tiny free-flowing, life-giving, crystal-clear cataract ...

and the robin comes to bathe –

      bird and human interact.

Let spring come again, we clamour, we demand, we humbly pray,

And then, through the mist, ever-brighter comes the low sun's ray.

And heaven and nature, earth and every living thing, sing.

      'Spring is coming!'

The deep winter darkness is giving way.

The robin takes wing; the sparrow, too, ere long

and my heart leaps as I remember the angel's command not to fear.

For the Creator will come – is already here

in nature's song, crisp and clear.

Teenage Life

A Stroke of Luck

Headmaster, Mr John Threadgold – aka Jack – stalked the corridors of his newly built 1950s boys' secondary modern school with the upright authority and aura of terror that he believed his profession demanded of him. If any of us boys – or the staff – were in doubt of our place in the hierarchy of his establishment, we were reminded by the swish of his cane as he beat it against his right trouser leg.

Jack was never without his cane. It rested on the front of his desk in full view of any boy or parent who was unfortunate enough to be summoned to his office. Do not assume, however, that it was merely for show; it was employed in anger several times a day. Boys were struck on legs, buttocks or hands in private or in public and the strokes duly recorded in the headmaster's logbook kept specifically for the purpose. At the end of each term, the frequency of the cane's application was entered into the formal report sent home to the parents. Some of them felt sympathy for their sons but, more often, anger that their progeny had 'let the family down'.

Such was the fate of Anthony Burton. He was an unfortunate boy in that his father cared more for drink and his elder sister, Rosie than him. Rosie knew how to manipulate her father – she quickly learned how to apply feminine appeal and became her daddy's girl. This worked well until, at sixteen, she took a boyfriend – but that's a different story.

As a male, Anthony, according to his father, was supposed to be red-blooded and his father deliberately bullied him in order to 'toughen him up'. Two things were guaranteed to annoy Anthony's father – reports that some other boy or boys had bullied his son or that he had been humiliated by the teachers. He instructed his son to stand up to his bullies and not ever to allow the Burton name to be debased.

'If anyone bullies you, son, hit them where it hurts. Hard! You're a Burton. Right?' commanded his father.

But Anthony was not blessed with a physique that could pack much of a punch and, besides, bullies operate in gangs. He was a loner – he did not have a gang – but he had to defend some place in the pecking order. If a Burton slipped into the bottom slot, his life would not be worth living. So he scanned the scene for those he deemed weaker than himself and bullied them in turn –

nothing involving bodily harm, something more subtle than that. He removed excise books from satchels, blotted boys' homework, told malicious tales and stole people's underwear in the changing rooms. I didn't like him – none of us did, even if he didn't do things to me, he was a creep. It was only later that I got to meet his father and to understand.

However, it was what Anthony did to Paul Smith's recorder that got him reported to Jack in the first instance. What he did need not be told in detail – suffice it to say that it was not nice. After that, we – all of us – took courage and reported him for the things he had perpetrated against anyone. And, of course, his bullying nemeses took advantage and dobbed him in for things he had not done. The result: a frequent flurry of the cane ... and the further corporal punishment inflicted by his father for causing shame to fall upon the Burton name. If Anthony had ever had any self-esteem, he had lost it now.

Anthony retreated into a world of his own. No longer a menace, we ignored him. I can look back on it now and realise we should have done something to help him but when you're only a teenager and worried about your own acceptance, it's difficult to think about others.

We later learned that he imagined scenarios in which he would become the hero – a superman whose identity was reluctantly revealed to the world. He would save screaming women from skyscraper ledges or outwit the criminal armed with a bomb – a device he would single-handedly defuse whilst the population held their breath. But there were no skyscrapers anywhere in our town and bomb-laden criminals were a rarity – in fact, we never heard of any. And, anyway, he couldn't fly, could he?

Perhaps, more realistically, like some kids, he could have scored a series of sixes and taken his side to victory. That would have done the trick – earned him a bit of respect. But the kind of kids who can do that are almost as rare as skyscrapers and he wasn't one of them. If he got to take his turn at the wicket, which he had only managed on a few occasions, it would be at number eleven and he'd have to face nasty deliveries either aimed at his head or arrowed at his feet – nothing he could score off, even if he had a batsman's talent, which he hadn't.

However, it turned out that he did have a most enduring fantasy to make his mark which, in hindsight was not going to help him. It would only have made matters worse but it is easy to say that now. Back then he was trapped and contemplating an act that would go down in history and gave him a sense of power that no one thought him capable of. Over several months, he devised a plan to set fire to the school. He would begin, he decided, with the headmaster's study.

Anthony had ready access to paraffin which the family used to fuel the free-standing stove – the sort that used to make the orange patterns on the ceiling – as well as candles, tapers and, of course, matches but the real opportunity would arise before bonfire night when fireworks were in ready supply. And that time was approaching. He would do it at night, of course, when no one was there to notice him. It never occurred to him that setting fire to a school might endanger life. Night after night for a whole week, Anthony went to sleep perfecting his plans. His fantasy both empowered and distracted him from the vicissitudes of the previous day.

After a particularly bad day in which he had once again found himself in the headmaster's office to be caned, Anthony decided to act on his fantasy. After the family had gone to bed, he rose, silently dressed and, taking his mother's black pack-a-mac so as not to be seen – a ruse planned in his reveries – the boy went to recky the school at midnight. He knew which way he was going to approach. He would scale the fence at the bottom of the playing fields and skirt the perimeter in the shadow of the trees which lined it. He hadn't thought about the moon but he was in luck – the sky was cloud-covered that night and the darkness was complete.

Anthony got to the asphalted area that surrounded the hall and turned the corner, keeping close to the wall outside the headmaster's office. The bottom of the window from the outside was shoulder height. Anthony looked in through the Venetian blinds. It was empty and dark but not so dark that he couldn't make out Mr Threadgold's cane.

In two weeks time, Anthony told himself, he would return with his incendiary equipment, break the window, pour in the paraffin, throw the can inside, light a sparkler, drop it in and leave in exactly the same manner as he was going to do now.

Anthony kept low and recrossed to the trees. Easy. He was almost at the end of the field but this time came too close to Mr Potts, the caretaker's, house that stood in the corner. A dog started to bark. A light came on and he saw Mr Potts framed in the upstairs window looking out to see what had disturbed his Alsatian. Instinctively, Anthony ducked down in the shadows. The dog was inside the caretaker's garden and could not get at him but Mr Potts had left the window and was probably already on his way down to the gate to let the dog loose. Anthony sprinted for the fence and was over it in a trice. It was easier from the inside because of the cross braces. He heard the dog barking in his trail so he crossed the road and hid behind a parked car. Looking through its window he saw Mr Pott's head appear over the fence but he came no further – he was not going to let his dog out onto the main road.

Anthony slunk off home. He was glad he had made the recky because, if he was going to do this for real, he was going to have to plan his getaway better, taking into account the dog. Once the school was on fire the alarm would be raised and he would be caught before he made it to the bottom of the playing fields, anyway. Could he devise something with a fuse that would give him time to get clear? He sauntered along, contemplating the problem. Avoiding getting caught had not formed a large part of his fantasy before and he did not like the feeling. He almost had been on this recky and it was scary. It spoiled things – he would not drift off to comfortable sleep now – unlike the fantasies, the realities were scarier. And he wasn't home yet; he was still outside at one in the morning when his parents believed he was in bed.

A hundred yards from his front door, however, a situation arose that was to change Anthony's life forever. A large man in a dark coat and flat cap was staggering down the pavement towards him. He appeared to be drunk. As the boy watched him he wondered how he was going to get by him without being seen but, to his relief, the man began to cross the road. A third of the way across, however, the man staggered and fell but he seemed to be all right because he was trying to get back onto his feet. Anthony hurried along to pass him but as he came adjacent to him, a car rounded the bend ahead at speed. The man was now back on his feet but swaying unsteadily. Anthony waited for the car to brake or swerve. It did neither. The man seemed quite unable to get out of the way; he was on his feet but only just. He seemed fixed, unable to make his legs move.

Anthony couldn't explain why he acted. He just did. He ran out towards the man and grabbed him by an extended arm and pulled. The man lurched towards him out of the path of the now screeching car but not quite far enough – a back wheel caught the man's foot before the car spun and slammed into a postbox on the opposite side of the road. A man got out of the driver's seat, keeping his back to Anthony, and disappeared between two houses. After all the noise, the silence was eerie. The man's flat cap lay several yards down in the road – scuffed and torn. If Anthony hadn't tugged the man out of the way, that would have been him as well as his cap. Anthony looked down at the man; he was alive and conscious – his hand was reaching towards his damaged foot. The boy just had time to register that he had probably saved the man from certain death when he saw who it was – Jack! And Mr Threadgold had clearly recognised the boy who was the latest victim of his cane. Not a face to forget.

The street filled quickly with residents and an ambulance came and took the headmaster to the hospital. Anthony was taken home by a policeman.

For three days after the incident, Jack didn't show up at school. We heard all sorts of rumours which got more and more exciting and extreme in the telling. Anthony said nothing. We had no idea he knew exactly what had happened; he just allowed all the fanciful speculation to spread.

Eventually, on the fourth day, the headmaster arrived using a pair of wooden crutches. He claimed the stage at the morning assembly. His cane was not in evidence; he couldn't hold both it and the crutches. He apologised for his absence, explaining that an idiot in a car had nearly killed him and sincerely hoped it was not a past pupil of the school. Apparently, the police had a good idea who it was but he was claiming the car had been stolen. Then, quite unexpectedly, he called Anthony forward. We fell completely silent – the kind of silence that only comes when not one boy is fidgeting with anything or even moving. What was he going to do to Anthony and why? Jack hadn't got his cane but he did have a pair of very sturdy wooden crutches!

The butterflies in Anthony's stomach must have become like a herd of elephants. You could see he was almost paralysed with fear but not quite because the fear had somehow anaesthetised his brain so that his legs could take him to his fate on the platform. It must have been like that for Charles I or Anne Boleyn. He knew what the assembled school would look like from the front – every single eye in the school would be upon him. The expectant hush deepened– no one even contemplated so much as a breath.

'Some of you, began Mr Threadgold, 'may not have heard of diabetes. It is a nasty disease that I suffer from. It is not catching, so you need not concern yourselves. In my case, it can on occasion – a very rare occasion – cause me to fall over. The other evening I was suffering from one of these rare falls in the road. I could have been killed by that idiot driver if Mr Burton, here, had not pulled me out of its path. I owe my life to this young man and I want to thank him publicly.' He began to applaud; the staff did likewise and, gradually, we all joined in. Some of those who hated Anthony the most were reluctant but eventually they did, too, as Mr Threadgold took an envelope from the lectern and handed it to Anthony. 'Here, young man, is my letter of commendation for your actions – the like of which I have never awarded a pupil before. Add this to your certificates of achievement which I have no doubt will be something to boast about when, in due time, you leave this school.'

Anthony looked up at him and managed to squeak his thanks; he left the stage as the school began the morning hymn.

It hadn't been difficult for Anthony to make up a story to explain his presence on the street in the middle of the night; he said he had gone out for a walk because he couldn't sleep. Mr Threadgold, it appeared, hadn't been drunk but had suffered an imbalance in his diabetes on his way home from a party. He had thought he could get home in time to remedy the situation but he had misjudged it. His foot was broken but was expected to heal without any lasting damage.

The thing Anthony never managed to explain was why he was wearing his mother's pac-a-mac ... especially as it wasn't raining and made him look rather stupid but every hero must have his secrets, I suppose.

A Young Man's Prayer

God, I feel crap!
I'm, like, in a trap.
And, before you say it,
it's a kinda prayer, innit?
I ain't faking;
I ain't taking
the Lord's name
like, in vain.
You know, I met this vicar.
(His name was Peter.)
He went, like, OMG
can mean, 'God come to me';
a call for real –
a prayer to heal.

So, God, I feel crap.
Are you gonna zap?
It ain't, like, nice;
it ain't a case of lice.
I wish God you would sort it –
I know how I caught it.
God, I feel crap.
Oh God, the *clap!*

And God goes:
'OK,
get to the doc's right away.
And don't forget, bruv
you have my undying love.
Always remember to give me your heart...
and, in future, get smart;
watch what you do with your ... part.'

Decisions

It's the day before my fourteenth birthday. I am sound asleep when Dad leaves for work. *Bang!* He never closes the front door quietly. *Slam!* That's the car door and then he revs the engine. The quicker we get an electric car the better!

I snuggle further down the bed. The bedroom's cold and dark – probably because it's February. I'm just going back to sleep when Mum bangs on the door and tells me it's time to get up. I ignore it.

'You awake, Louise?' she demands. If I don't answer she'll carry on banging.

'Yeah,' I say.

'Make a move, then.' Now I've got at least another fifteen minutes.

The next thing I know is Mum striding into the room and pulling back the covers. If I were not still half asleep, I could have said something that would have reduced my family credit score even further. I grab the duvet back around me and put my feet to the carpet and move slowly towards the door. Mum watches until I go into the bathroom leaving the bedding on the landing floor.

It is while I am washing that I remember that today is a non-uniform day. Bother! What the hell am I going to wear?

I go downstairs in my PJs. Mum's about to tear into me when I explain.

'What am I going to wear, Mum?' I demand.

'Well, anything,' she says, 'as long as it's decent.' 'Decent' means nothing that reveals a square inch of flesh. That is not helpful. Surely she should know that what you wear on a non-uniform day is absolutely vital. What you wear when you have a choice defines you. The thing is, I can't wear what others aren't because otherwise I'd stand out but if I wear *exactly* the same it will be a catastrophe. The safe thing is to be more daring than the others – just a tad. But that would be definitely vetoed by Mum – condemned as indecent. You see the problem.

I know what the others would be doing. They'd be on social media checking it out with each other. Me? Oh no. Mum outlaws the phone till after I'm dressed and have eaten my breakfast by which time it will be too late.

'Mum, can I have my phone so I can see what the others are wearing?' I ask in hope.

Mum thinks about it and then says, 'Sit down and eat your breakfast, then you can.'

'But Mum!...' It's no use. I sit down.

Breakfast is always a nightmare. Mum doesn't mind what I eat so long I eat a 'proper something'. I fancy the sugar-coated flakes ... but they are bad for the figure aren't they? Toast is worse, perhaps. Mum suggests eggs. *Eggs!* That will bring me out in spots, for goodness sake! And I haven't got time for them to cook in any case. I bolt the sugar puffs and sneak the toast to the dog when Mum's got her back turned.

Eventually, I get my phone. And guess what? The battery's completely flat! I take it back to the bedroom to find the charger. Where the hell is it?

After ten minutes I still haven't found it and if I don't get dressed now, I'm going to be late. Mum's already calling me down.

So I have to decide all by myself. Decisions! I hate decisions – especially important ones like this. Mum and Dad reckon my subject options are the most important but I can't take all the one's I want to take because they're all in the same column – drama, art, graphic design and textiles. On top of English and maths (which I'm rubbish at), I *have* to do a language – I'm doing French because Minnie and Josie are and I want to be with them. I *have* to do a science – yuk. I *have* to do a humanity – I can't stand geography and the history teacher's a nightmare. That leaves RS or business studies. And it turns out RS is oversubscribed and I've been given business studies! So not much choosing in the end, then. If I could really choose, I would go to theatre school but, of course, that's out of the question because it'd be boarding and fee-paying and Mum and Dad wouldn't countenance either.

Anyway – back to the immediate vital decision. I eventually settle on a plain top with the letters UCLA, blue jeans – suitably ripped at the knee – should I have a go at the thighs, too? Tricky one that – and dirty trainers... or should I wear my Doc Martins? The dirty trainers win.

I roll up outside school in the nick of time and then I spot them. Minnie has turned up in a really fetching outfit – a skirt with frills! And Josie is dressed, like, for a party. So my stuff, by comparison, is absolutely naff! It was Mum's fault – if only I had had access to my phone! I found the charger by the way; it was underneath the duvet! Mum's fault again – she put it back on the bed when I was in the bathroom. It was too late by then and I have had to leave the phone plugged in at home – a whole day without my phone! The entire day is going to be a nightmare!

I could bunk off. I'm not in the habit of doing it – in fact, I never have... yet. But Mary and Jane do it often, spending their day in the shopping centre even in their uniforms but today, I'm not in uniform, am I? Perfect.

Too late. Zac's spotted me. He's smiling at me in a way that makes my stomach twist and I remember that today's the day – non-uniform or not – to make a bid for the same science set he's going to be in next year. It's vital that I pass the test and impress Miss Falconham if I'm to stand a chance. I've already done my bit of trying to charm her and it seems to have worked because she's young and still quite, well, easy to impress. If I could just end up being his partner for the experiments... no telling where that will lead but the competition's hot... Yet he has just smiled in my direction. Perhaps he wants to go to UCLA one day – I know I do. Los Angeles! Just think how cool that would be.

Zac scoots off with his mates and I line up on my own. Minnie and Josie still haven't noticed me. It's, like, not having my phone overnight is getting me left out of the loop. They're so in touch all the time and I'm not there.

In class, they're sitting together and I might not even be in the same room. It could be the jeans and sweatshirt but they're not even looking for me.

We've been a threesome since primary school but now...

The day drags. I reckon I've no chance with the science. The test was insanely hard. I guess I'm just not in Zac's league. The worse thing is that Minnie and Josie take till lunchtime to even speak to me. I know they're planning stuff for later but they don't say. I feel like just dumping them. I mean, I know we go back, like, forever but why should I just take being left out?

It's five o'clock. I'm home alone. I've even done the English homework – how sick is that? Ten minutes at the maths and I'm done. My phone bleeps a text. It's Josie. She wants to know if I would like to go round hers – with Minnie – to watch a film. Her parents are going to be out and so is her elder brother so we could watch an '18' and not get into bother. She's sent the title so I look it up.

What the...! This one sounds like blood, drugs and kinky sex from beginning to end. Mum and Dad would be livid if they ever found out I watched *that*! And, really, do I want to watch it? The world news is bad enough without added gore but if I don't go, I'll definitely get left out of anything else. This is, like, a test.

What should I do? Life sucks. Things are just sooo, like, complicated.

I text Josie that I'll come but I'm going to have to get the 'say so' from Mum when she gets in. I shan't tell her that they plan to watch an 18 and that Josie's parents won't be in.

But it's Dad who comes home first. That's unusual. Something's wrong – I can see it in his face.

'What's up, Dad? Why are you home early?'

'Can't hide anything from you, can I?' He laughs. Come to think of it, if I can read him that easily, he might be able to read me about going to Josie's. I hope not. 'OK. I'll tell you,' he goes. 'Work's changing.'

'How do you mean?... You haven't got the sack, have you?'

'No. Not the sack, exactly. The London office is closing, though. They're transferring everything to Washington. They want me to stay – even give me a promotion but it'll mean moving to Washington.'

'Washington! As in, like, the United States! Cool!'

'No, I'm afraid not, Louise. Washington near Sunderland. In the North-East. It's where George Washington originally came from. It's a big place with houses almost up to Sunderland.'

'We'd have to move, then?'

'If I'm to keep my job, yes.'

'Up north?'

'Yes.'

'Sunderland? Isn't that by the sea?'

'It is but Washington's on the inland side of it. It's not a famous seaside town.'

'Stadium of Light.'

'What?'

'Stadium of Light – it's what they call the place Sunderland play their football.'

'How'd you know that?'

'Zac. A guy from school. He's keen on football. West Ham. He and his dad went there once to a game and I never forgot the name.'

'Zac? He's a friend?'

'Well... sort of. He sticks with the boys mostly.'

The door opens and Mum comes in. 'Hello, Dave. You're home early. What's...?' She looks at me and then him and then me again. I know what she's thinking. *Has he come home early because he was called out to me?* She's like that, Mum. She's scared I would do something that she doesn't like. As if... Well, I haven't *actually* got to Josie's, yet, have I? I'm as innocent as a dove.

Dad speaks up. 'Not a disaster Lynn but my offices are moving.' Mum relaxes. It's not me. He's home because of a work thing.

'I'll put the kettle on,' she goes.

As we drink the tea, Dad explains.

'The North-East! but that's miles away,' says Mum with a look of horror.

'Yeah,' says Dad. 'I'll start looking for another job but whatever I get, it'll probably mean a salary cut.'

'But if we moved to Sunderland, you said you may be getting a promotion?' checks Mum.

'Yes. That's true. And the cost of living in the North-East is considerably less than here, so—'

I interrupt before Mum can get in. 'You could, then, like, buy a big house with a ginormous garden and—'

'Have you two decided things before I even knew about this?' demands Mum.

'No. But I did tell Louise because she asked. She knew something was not right... Like you. She's growing up. She's getting wise, Lynn.'

Mum relaxed. 'What about Mum and Dad? If we're up north...?'

'They're not that near to us now, are they?'

'We haven't been for, like, months,' I put in.

'I know,' sighs Mum. 'Don't remind me. But you're right, Dave. It takes hours to get to Bedford.'

'Wrong side of London,' I say, 'I bet you could get a fast train down from Sunderland in not much longer.'

'You've got it all worked out, haven't you, Louise? What about your school – your friends?' asks Mum.

'I haven't got any anymore.'

'What about Minnie and Josie?' queries Dad.

'Dumped 'em,' I say. 'Well... sort of.'

'What?' goes Mum. 'Today?'

I nod. 'They haven't spoken to me all day, virtually. And Josie wants me to go round to hers tonight while her parents are out and watch *Nightmare Land* with Minnie. I don't want to. It's like, violent and stuff... and it's an 18 anyway.'

'What!!' goes Dad. 'You're not watching *that*!'

'Exactly. And if I don't go, *they*'ll dump *me*. So I'm dumping them, first.'

'Like I said,' breathes Dad, 'our kid's growing up and becoming wise. I'm proud of you, Louise.' I bask in his – what does Jane Austen call it? – approbation. Well, if I'm growing up, I might as well use big words, since I can.

'So, coming back to this job?' asks Mum, 'when do you have to answer by?'

'Next week. They've given me a week to think about it.'

It's obvious that Mum isn't going to make dinner just yet and I guess they want to talk about it without me – wise as I am.

'OK,' I say, 'I guess you've got a lot to talk about but don't worry about me. If you want to move to Sunderland, I'm up for it. Now, I've got stuff to do.'

When I get back to my bedroom, I text Josie.

'Checked out *Nightmare Land* and I don't want to watch it,' I say. Then I add, 'And you shouldn't, either. Count me out.' That last bit'll make her angry. She hates being told what to do. I doubt if she'll speak to me for a week.

So that's that. I went from nearly bunking off and to nearly going round to watch an 18 when I knew I shouldn't, to being commended for being wise and grown-up all in one day! That's my story.

We *have* moved to the north but it isn't Sunderland… and, by the way, I've got a real cool boy as a science partner – Robert. He's no Adonis – I mean he's not at all like Zac – but he's a science ace, which means our practicals kinda work and the teacher doesn't think I'm naff at it. She even gave me approbation! In fact, Robert's taught me so much that I think I'm actually getting it. So Louise the scientist, that's me! And the history teacher here is OK and so I'm doing history and not business studies. Things are looking up.

But just in case you think you know who I am and want to pass this bit of a confession to my parents, then I have to tell you that I have changed the names of all the people in the story. I haven't used my own actual name, either! After all, I might end up by becoming a celebrity one day and I wouldn't want the twittersphere set ablaze with too many revelations, would I?

Called by Name

It was Maundy Thursday afternoon. The children were at home from school for their Easter holidays, and the church secretary was in a hurry to finish her work. The trouble with working for the church was that holidays – especially Christmas and Easter – were some of the busiest periods. She had just two tasks to complete – a booklet for a wedding on Easter Monday and a sheet for the readers at the Easter sunrise service; she would use her computing skills to do them quickly. She linked the two; they would print off one after the other with one instruction. On her computer, she selected the file of a previous wedding booklet. All that was needed was to change the names, and draught in the new hymns. She was so used to this and, with two strokes, all the references to 'John', the former groom, became 'Wayne', and all those to 'Mary', the former bride, became 'Lucy'. She checked it had worked: 'I, Wayne, take you, Lucy...' perfect. She sent the documents to the copier, which rattled them off, putting them into two separate piles. She pigeon-holed them, and then rushed home to her children.

Being thirteen can be a trying thing – especially being the daughter of enthusiastic Christian parents. Lucy was as tall as her mother but her body was outstripping her energy. She didn't mind going to church – well mostly – but she resented having to get up at five o'clock to go to this Easter sunrise service, which meant walking to an exposed cliff-top in freezing rain. Even if it wasn't cloudy, you never saw the sun itself – it just got light. It was mostly about braving the cold wind and the rain.

'Do I have to go?' moaned Lucy. 'It's boring. And it's public ... and the weather's foul.'

'It's about Jesus being alive again,' answered her father. 'Despite the weather, it's a sunrise service – bringing a little 'Sonshine' into your life ... S-O-N shine. Get it?'

'Duh! Dad! You know that's so naff.'

Watching Lucy arrive, the minister caught sight of her disdainful body language. He thought he could make her feel wanted by asking her to read the lesson. Her parents were delighted – Lucy was trapped. Her younger brother snickered. He knew exactly how well this was going down with his sister. She shot him a withering glance that was not in the spirit of Easter. Lucy took the paper she was given in her gloved hand. It was still rather dark, and she could barely read it but she thought she had better look through the reading if she was going to do it. There was no point in making a fool of herself. She got it close to her face. It was the story of Mary Magdalene in the garden when she found the tomb empty and then met the risen Jesus. Lucy knew it well but she ran through it anyway.

When she got to the bit where Jesus makes himself known, Lucy couldn't believe what she was seeing:

'Jesus said to her, "Woman, why are you weeping? Whom are you looking for?" Supposing him to be the gardener, she said to him, "Sir, if you have carried him away, tell me where you have laid him, and I will take him away." Jesus said to her, "Lucy!" She turned and said to him in Hebrew, "Rabbouni!"(which means Teacher).'

Lucy read it again. Were her eyes playing tricks on her? The name should be 'Mary' but the more she stared, the more she saw, 'Lucy'. Was God trying to tell her something? She had a vision of Jesus standing there on this exposed cliff-top, looking straight into her eyes, and saying, 'Lucy!'

Lucy felt small and embarrassed. *This is definitely, like, my mind playing tricks on me,* she told herself. Yet, even if it was, if you believed in Jesus and that he died on the cross and was raised for you, he *did* call you by name. She remembered the words of the bishop at her confirmation service six months before: 'I have called you by name, you are mine.' (It was a quote from the Old Testament somewhere.) And now, here was Jesus, calling her by name just as he had Mary Magdalene in the garden on that first Easter day.

Mary hadn't wanted to be there in the graveyard that morning, anymore than Lucy wanted to be at this service. She was there because she had to be – because she loved Jesus so much. And Mary had been called by her name! Amazing – Jesus was alive. It had made the whole world a different place for her. And, now, here was this same Jesus making the world a different place for Lucy. He knew her and was calling her by her name. *Wow! That's, like, cool,* she thought. And then, *Thanks, Jesus. I love you too – honestly – even on this grotty morning.*

The service began. Lucy read the passage, substituting the name, 'Mary', although the paper still read, 'Lucy'. No one else seemed to have noticed.

The service was followed by breakfast in the chapel on the beach – the best part of the whole thing. It was here that she noticed the reference to the reading. In small letters underneath, it read: 'The Gospel according to St Wayne, Chapter 20, verses 1-18'.

Lucy laughed out loud. The sunshine had definitely broken through. The Son had risen! Alleluia!

Future Game

Tom sighed. This was just the thing he could do without right now. Dave, the youth leader, had come up with a game that involved pinning a piece of paper to people's backs and arming everyone with a pencil and a paper clip.

'OK,' said Dave. 'What you do is find someone – anyone – and write on the bottom of the piece of paper on his or her back a quality you associate with them – something they're good at. Fold it over so that no one else can see it and secure it with the paper clip. Now find someone else and do it again above the fold.' Dave showed them an example of one that he had done earlier. 'Make sure you don't write too big so as to leave plenty of room for everyone... oh, and you can only write on each person once! There are twelve of you, so leave room for twelve lines.'

Great, thought Tom who was feeling yuk, *that's all I need*. Tom was a musician – a pretty good one. So good that he had recently auditioned for a performing arts college – a place he had dreamed of from being thirteen. His parents were dead keen on it, too, but he had fluffed it – well, not exactly fluffed it; he was simply turned down. Turned down! The interviewer said that they were pleased with what they had heard but it was not quite what they wanted. Tom was gutted. That was two weeks ago, and now this.

Meanwhile, on the other side of the room, Skye was also dreading the exercise. Unlike Tom, who, she thought, was super-talented, Skye felt she had very little in the way of accomplishments. She couldn't play an instrument – couldn't even seem to sing in tune. Her father said she didn't have any rhythm and had given up trying to teach her to dance. Her parents were ballroom dancing champions but Skye was, in her father's words, a 'disappointment'. In fact, Skye didn't shine anywhere – she was in the bottom set for English, maths and science. Some of the kids at the youth centre were cool – but Skye had long since given up on trying to impress anyone. She only went along to the club because she liked Dave, and because she also loved Jesus who, like her, seemed to have got on the wrong side of people and got into trouble. She thought of Jesus as her friend; she didn't tell anyone of course because it would sound naff. She had talked to Jesus for years – and, somehow, she felt he liked her for some reason: so she persisted with the church club where the kids were certainly kinder to her than most of the others at school. Yet this game was stupid. Who would write anything nice on her back?

The game began. She looked around to find someone. Ron had been kind to her, so she turned him around and wrote: 'kind and gentle'. She was just pinning up his paper when she felt someone write something on her back. She couldn't see who it was. Then she spotted Tom. His back was free. Skye liked Tom. Once when they were on a picnic, Tom had waited for her while everyone else had finished and had gone to play football. Tom had just talked while she chomped and Skye had thought that was nice. She wanted to write 'thoughtful' but she couldn't remember how to spell it. She shrugged and put: 'payshunt'.

The game continued until everyone had written on everyone else's back. Dave sat them all down in a circle and asked if they would like to see what people had written. They could just take the papers home if they didn't want to look now.

'No time like the present,' said John, who was popular and couldn't wait to see what nice things people had to say about him. Soon everyone was looking at their papers. Skye began to cry. Instinctively, Tom put his arm around her shoulders. 'It's alright Skye. What have they said? Is it all wrong?'

'No,' sobbed Skye, 'it's quite the opposite,' she whispered.

Tom looked at his paper. 'Wow! He hadn't realised how much people appreciated him. He read: 'good listener', 'loves old people', 'never gives up', 'thinks of others', 'great smile', 'quiet and ace'. He knew who had written that. To John, everything was either 'ace' or 'yuk'. He smiled at him. Tom had written, 'cheers you up' on his back.

At the end of the session, Tom told Skye the game had settled his future.

'How'd you mean?' asked Skye.

'I thought I wanted to become a musician in some great orchestra – or even a soloist but having read these things I know what I am going to do. I am not going to reapply for a performing arts course, I am going to go to clearing to see if I can get into teaching.'

'You would be a great teacher!' exclaimed Skye immediately. 'You're so wonderful with kids and you're so patient. My dad told me I couldn't sing but you got me to learn that thing we all had to do last Sunday, and I did it. You made me believe I could do it.'

'You *can* sing. Don't believe those who say you can't.'

'After that game, I think I know what I'm going to do, too,' smiled Skye. 'I'm going to work in the old people's home. The manager has already asked me but I wasn't sure I could do it.'

'But now you are? You'd be good ... Great! So you're going to work with the old folk and I with the young ... You know, I was dreading that game.'

'So was I ... That's Dave's gift isn't it?'

'Yeah, he knew we needed a boost. He's so wise.'

'Yeah. And cool.'

It's Just Not Fair!

'It's just not fair!' said Melanie, angrily.

'What's not fair?' asked her brother, Andy.

'Everything. You know, the world, school, life... everything.'

'Does that include me?'

'Well, sometimes... but not mostly.' Melanie laughed. She was fond of her brother.

'Thanks.' Andy smiled. 'So some things are all right. What about your friend, Pippa?'

'She's OK. Great actually. I'm glad she's my friend.'

'And Adele?'

'Adele?' quizzed Melanie. 'Oh, you mean *Adele*.' She mimed a microphone and sang, 'You know she's my idol.'

'And what about Miss Quant at school? You said the other day that she was cool.'

'Yeah, She is, mostly... OK. How many others can you think of who are all right?'

'What about Jesus?'

'Oh, I give up! OK. Well perhaps not *everyone* sucks, not *everything*. Only most things.'

Andy didn't say anything for a whole minute. He was thinking. His sister was right. Despite all the good things, a lot of things in the world sucked. He thought of the pictures on the news. Wars, murders, celebrities who had taken advantage of kids for years without anyone doing anything to stop them, the way big business was wrecking the climate...

'Wouldn't it be great,' he said wistfully, 'if we could just, like, wave a magic wand and all the bad things would disappear?'

'Yep. But some of the things *I* think suck, Mum and Dad think are not so bad. Maybe they'd stop the magic happening ... like they stop us doing so many things. Dad keeps saying, 'That's not for you to worry about, Melanie – you just concentrate on your school work'... Lot's of things are stopped by adults... And anyway, I haven't got a magic wand – nobody has.'

'But there must be something we could do if things go wrong, or are bad or not fair?' insisted Andy. 'It seems, well, kind of wrong just to complain to each other about things but never do anything.'

'Yeah. But the world is cram full of adults and people who just want their own selfish way. They'd never listen to us. We're just kids who are to be seen and not heard. You know what Greta Thunberg got called? A brat.'

Andy thought for a moment.

Perhaps. Yet there *must* be *something* we could do. There just has to be... That's it. I've made up my mind, I'm joining the strike.'

'You mean the school strike? but you can't; you know what the headteacher said. It'll go on your report and Mum and Dad'll go mental.'

'I don't care. If Greta can do it, so can I!'

'But Greta's Greta. She's different.'

'Is she? That's just the point. She's only different because she sat outside the school on strike and the world listened. Why? Because she's a teenager – like us.'

'Right. You mean teenagers have power?'

'Exactly. Grown-ups want to keep us down because they want to stay in control or because they're scared and don't want to draw attention to themselves or because they want to protect us or something but I don't care. I don't care about the head and I don't care if Mum and Dad don't like it.'

'Andy!'

'OK, Mel. Tell me I'm wrong.'

'I... I can't. You... might be the only kid on strike.'

'So? Greta was on her own when she began.'

'But... but... if you do it, you won't be on your own. If you do it, so will I. And so will a bunch of others we know. They're just waiting for someone to be first... And then, maybe, our parents will be proud of us. Scared maybe but proud – like Greta's dad.'

And so it turned out. Andy and Melanie's Mum and Dad supported them. They were pleased that they cared and didn't mind them going on strike, so long as they stayed together, kept safe and let them know exactly where they were and what they were doing. They even helped them find the materials to make their banners.

When Greta came, the city centre was packed with young people calling for change – and the schools were closed for the day and the people standing for election to the seats of power were seeking the green vote … And Andy and Melanie's proud parents are calling for people to listen to their teenagers.

Two Gardens

There was once a rich widower who retired into a lovely house surrounded by a beautiful garden. He hadn't lived there long, however, before he discovered that also in the neighbourhood there were some teenagers for whom life in the village was rather dull. They had no transport to the town, so they amused themselves by running around and generally making a nuisance of themselves.

One weekend, the rich man discovered them in his garden and chased them away. When they returned, he built a fence, which didn't keep them out for long. Next he built a wall, which worked for a few days but which soon became an interesting challenge for the kids – finding a way over was fun. Finally, he topped the wall with broken glass and razor wire and threatened them with a shotgun. After that, the teenagers gave up and no one came to see him at all, not even the adults in the village. The beautiful garden became a lonely place for him.

Eventually, he became too ill to tend his garden properly and it became overgrown and derelict, a place where the sun could not penetrate; it was no longer beautiful but dark and gloomy like the sad man who owned it.

At about the same time, in a village up the road, a retired gentleman of more modest means moved into a cottage. It was blessed, however, with a large garden with half a dozen fruit trees and several vegetable beds, as well as flower borders. The previous owner had employed a gardener but that was beyond the new owner's means. And he had to admit that, he, himself, was no gardener. Something had to be done, he told himself. He prayed to God; God would know what to do.

He had only been in the house for a couple of days, however, when he, too, discovered the roaming teenagers; the fruit trees were a great temptation. The problem wasn't just the stolen apples and plums but the trodden vegetables and broken fence. However, the gentleman gave thanks to God for the answer to his prayer.

The following day he recruited his neighbour and together they baked and iced cakes and sweet treats. Among the fruit trees, they erected a table and filled it with all they had made, along with fruits of every kind. When the young people arrived to do their habitual misbehaving they found the table with a note on it. It said: 'Welcome to my garden. It is open to you and all comers at any time but please look after it and tend it. This is for you. Enjoy!'

The teenagers couldn't believe what they were seeing. Surely this wasn't for them. They were confused and left without climbing a tree, trampling the vegetables or taking anything at all.

The day after they returned but found the table laid anew. This time the note read: 'To my regular young visitors – this is for you!' Something didn't feel right and they kept away.

The gentleman, however, was not about to give up. He had found an effective way of keeping his thieves out but that hadn't been his intention, so he went into the streets of the village with invitations for people to visit his garden whenever they wanted. Word went around that he actually liked people, including teenagers.

Soon people of all sorts came and accepted his hospitality. Of course, people brought as well as took and by the time the leaves were falling, local horticulturalists were offering to prune and prepare the vegetable beds for sowing. Skilled gardeners used the garden to teach the youngsters the arts of pruning and planting. The garden became a buzz of people – a paradise of shared knowledge and laughter. So the gentleman delighted in seeing, not only his garden blossom but the young people of the community, too. Now they had an absorbing interest in their village.

The gentleman of modest means had become rich with the care and love of neighbours and children. His next task was to persuade the recluse down the lane to remove his razor wire. The poor man may have had much wealth but he knew nothing of the joy of being part of things or seeing bored teenagers rejoicing in great things to do. How do you persuade the sad and beleaguered rich to enjoy the freedom and joy of belonging?
The problem is one without an easy solution. It's an age-old dilemma that even keeps God out.

Families

Dan's Dad

'Ooh, Dad, you'd be brilliant!'

'Do you really think so, Dan? I mean, what would your friends think if they knew your father was a parent school governor?'

'I don't care... I think it's, like, cool.'

That clinched it. I would allow my name to go forward for election. Several people, including our friends at the church and the youth leader, thought I could 'make a difference'. *I* wasn't so sure – but I do want to do something that would make things better for people – especially young people. If Dan at thirteen thought it was 'cool', then all the excuses I could muster seemed irrelevant.

Three weeks later.

'... And finally, before we go into the head's report,' announced the chair of governors, Sir Joseph Trimshaw, 'may we welcome Mr Derek Plumber our new parent governor.'

I forced a smile and raised my hand awkwardly in acknowledgement. I felt completely overawed by the august membership of the school's governing body, where most of the members seemed to have prefixes other than a simple Mr, Mrs or Miss. Even the teacher governor to my left, a young woman who exuded perfumed confidence, had signed against the name Mx Samantha Crowther.

Sir Joseph called upon the head to make his report.

'Governors,' Dr Trench began, 'I won't spend long on unnecessary details...' Ten minutes later he was still on his feet. I was struggling to follow any of it. He spoke in gobbledygook but he didn't sound that happy. How on earth I was going to be useful on this body, I couldn't imagine.

'... So you see,' he concluded, 'the unfortunate GFTs have affected our KANGA rating, and added to the HTC staff FDN, we are at risk of finding ourselves under SSM from the GTFA within the next six months. So I am proposing that we apply for DGF. This is item 5a on your agenda.' He sat down – there was silence except for a few creaking chairs and a clunk, which turned out to be Mx Sam's high-heeled shoe falling off.

'Thank you, Dr Trench,' said Sir Joseph.

Mx Sam uncrossed her legs and began searching for her shoe with her foot, inadvertently kicking me in the leg.

'Sorry,' she whispered. Dr Trench looked at her, then me, over his half-moon glasses, as you would expect a headmaster to.

Councillor Downs, the treasurer, circulated six A4 pages of double-sided columns of figures which made no sense to me at all. 'Don't worry,' whispered Mx Sam, 'they'll become clearer in a year or two.' I nodded. I kept my head down just in case the half-moon specs were directed at our corner again. Councillor Downs told us that the five-figure minus number on page six was only a notional sum, and not to be alarmed at. The governors breathed a collective sigh of relief. 'And,' he smiled approv-ingly, 'if we are granted DGF then money comes with it... Any questions?'

Why I did it, I don't know. Perhaps it was an attempt to show that I was not a complete idiot but, if so, it backfired.

'May I ask what is the DGF?' I asked. Stares from around the table bore into me.

'No doubt you will have seen the glossary in the governors' handbook,' said Sir Joseph. 'New governors soon pick it up. It might be useful to have it open in front of you in the first few meetings... Page sixty-seven.'

'Er, thanks,' I said, hoping that the floor would open up beneath me. *Why on earth did I take this on? 'Make a difference'... you must be joking?* All this was totally out of my league.

'Well,' asked Dan, when I got in. 'Do they know what's wrong with the school, then?'

'What do you mean, 'What's wrong?''

'Oh. Don't be dense, Dad. You know what. The place is totally failing and sinking into a hole the size of China... only China's richer.'

'Governors' meetings are confidential, Dan.'

'Yeah but just tell me whether they know... they *do* know, don't they? If you ask me, they want more of the, like, 'ities' and less of the 'shuns'.'

'What *are* you talking about? I don't think I should need to have a glossary to understand my own son!'

'Oh, Dad. They *have* given you a rough time, haven't they?... The 'ities' are those words that end in 'ity'. Like 'generosity', 'jollity', 'vitality', 'authenticity'... The 'shuns' are words like 'oppression', 'obsession', 'depression', 'station'...'

'Station?'

'Yeah. As in: "Get to know your station, boy. Don't get cocky."'

'I hope you don't cheek your teachers, Dan Plumber!'

'Only if they lack the 'ities'. We like Mx Sam because she has 'integrity' but Tricky Trench oppresses everyone to profit his own ambi*tion*.' Dan laughed, 'I will grant you he has one 'ity' though - 'pomposity'.'

'Dan! That's rude... Dr Trench works extremely hard for you and all the students. If I have learned one thing, it is that he really cares about the school – even if he seems to be on a different planet most of the time. You have to be jolly clever to be a headteacher in today's world ...'

The next day I re-read the governor's handbook, and then the minutes of the previous meetings. For all the big words, initials and acronyms, I was beginning to get the picture. I am sure they *do* know what's going on. I have gathered that the school is in a bit of a financial and quality depression that Dr Trench is attempting to address. The poor man. Things are not as bad as Dan makes out, of course – but there *are* challenges which I think I can help the governors address – when I get the hang of it. It's going to be hard work – but one thing I have learned above all is that working with a school means you are on the front line in the community. If I can do something that would help just one child, it would be worth it.

And as for Dan, I am going to encourage him to engage in some less pressured activities alongside the serious stuff; perhaps involving Personal Learning And Young, Independent, Non-directed Growth (PLAYING).

Dad Grows Up

'Dad! Do you have to?' Anya squirmed. She looked around desperately hoping none of her friends was looking in his direction. No such luck; best friend, Kirsty, had definitely seen her dad's mocking gyrations poking fun at the dance music they were downloading. She caught Kirsty's attention, then puckered her face and rolled her eyes in a show of disbelief. Kirsty returned a similar knowing look. She was sympathetic – after all her own father was more than a little embarrassing with his penchant for dismantling old motorbikes and leaving the drive scattered with oily engine innards.

'One day, Anya Fortnam, you'll be grateful for your old man,' her father responded as he removed himself to the kitchen.

'One day, like, a million years from now, ' muttered Anya, too quietly for him to hear but not so discrete he didn't get the message. She shared a forced conspiratorial laugh with Kirsty. That her father heard; he knew it was at his expense and he grinned.

The next morning, Frederic Fortnam dropped Anya off at school – or rather a block from the school; she didn't want to be seen in his car.

'Don't worry. I'm getting a new one,' he announced.

'A new what?'

'A new state-of-the-art car. When you see it you'll want me to drive you right up to the school. Cool, eh?'

'Do you think it's the car I'm ashamed of?' Anya blurted. She opened the car door, got out and uttered a 'See ya,' and disappeared. As she went she rolled her eyes; she seemed to be doing a lot of that these days when her dad was around.

Frederic shrugged off her discouragement. *Teenagers!* His mood had improved when he thought of the new car he was planning to treat himself to, and work was a place where he was respected, especially by his personal assistant, Lisa.

When he arrived, he found Lisa already there, eager to impress. Her career depended on it – being a PA was, she hoped, just a beginning. With an air of efficiency, she held out a folder.

'Mr Fortnam. Your hard copies,' she said. 'The ones you ordered.' She exchanged the file for his coat which she hung carefully on a stand.

'Thank you, Lisa,' he said with a smug smile. 'Excellent.'

'You're welcome,' she replied as her boss continued into his inner office.

As lunchtime approached, Lisa looked for the hard copy of the email from her boyfriend that she had printed off with the details of their planned holiday; she needed it to get some foreign currency during her lunch break but it was not where she expected it to be. She searched everywhere including under her desk. Nothing. The only possibility she could think of was that it had got into Mr Fortnam's folder! Damn! It wouldn't have been the end of the world if it weren't for her boyfriend's calling her Bunnykins and ending the email with a line of 'x's and 'o's.

She was still blushing at the thought as Frederic Fortnam opened his door, held up the email and said with a dignified air covering a tone of contemptuous triumph. 'I don't think this is intended for me, Lisa.' Frederic admired his perfectly executed put down.

'S ... sorry.' Lisa stammered. She winced. If only the floor would open up so she could fall through. After a barely concealed leer, her boss went back inside. *Ouish!* she thought. How much had he read? *All of it – probably twice over!*

It wasn't yet midday and Frederic Fortnam had already scored twice on the cringe chart. He had deliberately made fun of his daughter with his mocking dance and had now caused his PA to blush. What power! What a triumph! So why was something deep inside him beginning to make him feel uncomfortable? He tried to shrug it off – if people were embarrassed that was their problem, wasn't it? After all, Anya's music was really naff and Lisa had been negligent – Bunnykins of all names! Yet something was telling him that it *wasn't* all right. As he sat at his desk, he became confused. It was only a game; he didn't want to actually upset people – just tease them. Why were these girls so sensitive? He swore to himself.

Lunchtime came and Frederic left his office for the pub he usually frequented. That day, however, it was crowded with young men in their early twenties – probably on some office convention. They were well lubricated for a lunchtime and spilt out onto the pavement. As Frederic approached, half considering to go elsewhere that day, a young woman hurried down the pavement towards him; she had a bag on her arm and a coffee in her hand. In an attempt to avoid the mêlée, she stepped off the curb but caught her heel and lost her balance. She fell. Her bag hit the road scattering papers, and her coffee shot into the air.

Along with the young men, Frederic's first reaction was one of amusement. Some of the young men made unseemly remarks. None made any move to help. It was then that something happened to Frederic Fortnam. It was as if a sack of understanding burst inside his head; suddenly he perceived the woman's humiliation. He felt an empathy that he had not experienced before and he cringed *for* her. Something had opened his eyes and he found himself becoming angry!

'Get some manners!' he barked at the useless jeering young drinkers.

Heedless of his own dignity, he chased up the road after the papers that the wind was taking – he even stopped a van and a cyclist to retrieve a loose A4 sheet that had strayed into their path. He didn't give up until he had retrieved the last sheet just before it disappeared under a bus. He collected them together as neatly as he could and presented them to the young woman who was now standing on one foot rubbing her ankle. She thanked him profusely.

'Are you all right?' he asked, genuinely concerned.

'Y... yes, I think so,' she answered. 'I don't think I have done anything serious to it.' She put her foot down and tested it. 'Yeah. It's OK... Thank you. Thank you so much for collecting my paperwork.'

'I think it's all there. It's all mixed up, though.'

'That's OK. It's nice to know that there still are some caring people about,' she smiled, looking at the group of half-inebriated delegates.

'Just ignore that lot. They've still got some growing up to do... Your coffee. Let me get you another.' The woman protested but Frederic made to cross to the coffee shop. 'What will it be? Cappuccino?' He ordered the coffee and touched his card. 'For the lady.' He nodded to her, smiled and then left – he did not want to cause her further embarrassment.

At five o'clock, as Lisa got ready to leave, Frederic managed, at last, to say what he had wanted to all that afternoon. He took courage.

'Lisa, I'm sorry.'

'What for Mr Fortnam?'

'Embarrassing you this morning. It was wrong of me.'

For a moment Lisa felt as if she might blush anew but immediately sensed her boss's sincerity.

'Thank you,' she said. 'Apology accepted.' Perhaps she had misjudged Mr Fortnam.

On his way home, Frederic pondered his day. It had certainly felt good when he had had that impulse of empathy, seeing things from the other person's point of view. Now he felt bad about Anya – teenage years were not that easy. He remembered his own. Perhaps if he treated her as more grown-up rather than as a big kid he might embarrass her less. In fact, he should stop thinking of her as a big kid – who knows what young adult sentiments were going on in her heart and mind these days.

As they sat down for tea, he addressed her as if she were his equal – a fellow adult. He asked, 'Anya, about changing the car. What do you think? Should I?'

Anya stared at him. She couldn't detect any sarcasm. 'You really, like, honestly want my opinion, Dad?'

'Yes, I do.'

'Honestly?'

'Yes.'

'Frankly, a new car would be an unnecessary luxury. The old one's OK. There's nothing wrong with it.'

To Anya's amazement, that seemed to be the end of the matter; no new car arrived. For some reason, her dad had changed. She had no idea why but she liked it. And she decided not to roll her eyes anymore when grown-ups were mentioned. That was, like, childish, wasn't it? And she wasn't a child anymore, was she?

The Worlds Inside the House in Squirrel Square

Squirrel Square

Edwardian redbrick
Brass knocker
Oak bannisters
Polish
Home
Kitchen
Kettle
Bread and fresh grown veg
White wooden loo seat
Big blue bath
Fluffy feather beds
Home amidst the city's unknown throng
Soft sofas arranged around cast iron hearth
Safe at home at home at home at home...

Mum's World

Lawnmower
Tubs
Geraniums
Lilac

Pots

Strawberries
Compost bin
Daffodils
Cherries
Close clipped hedge
Potted begonias spilling scarlet blooms
Beautiful bird bath lovingly scrubbed and

Pots and pots and pots and pots....

Dad's World

Garage
Oil
Spanners
Drill
Bits
Hammers
Saws
Paint brushes
Sawdust strewn workbench
Half made wooden frame
Classic motor-bike in bits
Old fashioned moth-eaten Prams

in bits and bits and bits and bits ...

Grandma's World

Reclining chair
Magazines
Scented Soap
Knitting patterns
Pins
TV remote (x 5)
Trolley
Teapot beneath its cosy
Scattered sugar
Cat stalked budgie
Needles and Pins
Poof battered and loved harbouring

lost pins and pins and pins and pins....

Grandpa's World

Newspapers
Pens
Glasses
Port
Books
Humbugs
Slippers
Walking sticks
Scarves in summer
Pantomime Pictures
Cricket books
Encyclopaedias opened and stacked
with **books** and **books** and books and books...

Boy's World

Toy cars
Metal aeroplanes
Plastic truck
Dinosaur Duvet
Lego
Ice Cream
Scattered Marbles
X-box
Lunch box (mouldy)
Single smelly trainer (other lost)
Wind-up lego train
Discarded treasured teddy bear
and Lego and Lego and Lego and Lego ...

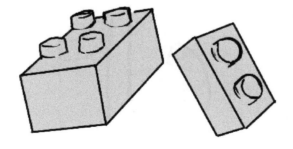

Teenager's World

Chocolate
Clothes
McDonald's trophies
Makeup

Homework

Sport's kit
Computer for online learning
Boy-band pictures
Bike helmet
TikTok, Instagram and Snapchat
Homework files
Hairbrushes, combs and scrunchies

and Homework and homework and homework and homework...

... and looming exams!

Family World

Weekends
The Beach
Birthdays
Cake
Love
Christmas at Squirrel Square
Bedtime stories
Church on Sundays
Toad in the Hole
Arrival of a new family pet
Mum's best pudding baked with love
Child's sponsored run in driving rain

Surrounded, bonded by love and love and love and God-given love!

Letters to Mami

Sometimes having to write thank-you letters can be a challenge for children. Here are two such letters. In both cases, they are letters to a French grandmother – Mami. How cool to have family in more than one country – or is it? Read on. We begin with the story of Annabelle's letter.

Annabelle's Letter to Mami

OK. So there's nothing, like, out of the ordinary about having to write to your grandmother. I know many kids have to do it. It's, like, your grandmother (who is never interested in what *you* find cool about the world and doesn't care about the things that you care about) has this thing about *you*. I mean she has to be so personal – always on about the way you behave, what you wear, how well you perform at school, the emergence of 'family values' and stuff. So she gives you something for your birthday that she thinks you ought to have, rather than want.

Well, my grandmother is French. I mean she's, like, lived in the same village in Normandy all her life. When he grew up my father somehow escaped to Paris where he met my mother (who comes from Bristol) and fell in love. Apparently, Mami (that's what I have to call her) went ballistic; but Dad embraced the opportunity of being free – not just from all things Lower Normandy but all things French too. Mami was not amused. The English are in second place only to the Germans in terms of undesirable foreigners. Her hero is Napoleon – who she reckons history has totally misunderstood. And she keeps banging on about *laicité* – whatever that means.

Well, Mami has never visited us in Bristol but we have to go to her home twice a year – and it's, well, frankly boring. Me and my sister just have to sit around, be good… and speak French to Mami, who is constantly sighing at the fact that however well we do… well, we're just not French! Then it's, '*Allez jouer!*' most of the rest of the time – she doesn't really want us around except as '*enfants pour la succession 'Dubois'*. As far as I can work out, Dubois is not a line that's on the brink of dying out – except, of course, in Mami's village. In any case, being female, when I marry – if I do and that's not a definite thing – I'll no longer be Dubois, will I? It's the best thing about getting married.

There are only two other children our age who live in Mami's village – brothers. It was OK when we were small but now I'm thirteen I don't particularly want to 'play' with spotty French *petits garçons* who are not *petits* these days. Actually, I reckon Mami has a secret hope that me and my sister will somehow fall in love with these brothers, and abandon all the world to come and live back in the ancestral village. No chance! It's not that the Dubois family (i.e. Mami) owns a *château* or anything – just a small *chaumière* – that's a thatched cottage – which is on the point of falling down, Dad says. Anyway, I'm not going to marry for ages – I want to go places – places that some of my school friends get to go to on their holidays – and beyond.

But, coming back to this letter. I have to write to Mami to thank her for the broach she sent me for my birthday. It's an ugly bronze caste of Marianne (like in the French version of Britannia) and the words, *Liberté, Égalité* and *Fraternité*. Does Mami think I'm ever going to wear it?! Some hopes. The thing is, I have to write in French. I ask you? How many kids of thirteen outside France have to do this? I begin, as always, '*Chère Mami. Je t'écris pour te remercier pour ton cadeau formidable. Il prendra la place d'honneur dans ma boîte à bijoux...*' *poubelle* more like!

And now for Louise's letter...

Louise's Letter to Mami

My father is French. This is cool because it means me and my sister have got to speak French from being little. When I moved up to secondary school, I didn't have French lessons like the others in my class but was given French books to read that some of the students were studying for GCSE. The teacher didn't expect me to write essays on them like the year elevens but just enjoy them. He also used me to help the others in spoken French – cool.

Anyway, my Dad's mother lives in Normandy, and I'm just writing her a letter to say thank you for my birthday present. She lives on her own and loves to come over and visit us in Bristol. She's always here for Christmas because she says it isn't fair that we should have to go to her when Santa Claus is bringing us our presents at home but we do go to her for 6th January if we can, because in Normandy that is *Le Fête des Rois* when the three kings arrive at the crib. The village has a big party that always has a special apple pie with a bean in it. If you get the bean you get to be the king or queen of the feast. My Dad got the bean last year and they gave him a cardboard crown; then he chose me to be his queen and we sat on special chairs.

There are not many kids living in the village but next door to Mami is a family living in a converted barn with two boys the same age as me and my sister. On Sundays, at the church, we sit with them and go out with them to a Sunday school that's kind of fun but now we're thirteen, the eldest invited me to go with him to a youth club in the town. I felt a bit awkward. Their French was kind of hard at first but the leader made a fuss of me and I was given loads of French stuff to eat. The French know how to eat. Dad says, '*En Grande-Bretagne on mange pour vivre, mais en France on vit à manger!*' As far as I can make out, it's almost true.

Mami is a great present buyer. You can get stuff in France you can't in the UK. I look forward to the parcel coming every year. Sometimes there are fantastic chocolates, other years you can tell it's toiletries before you open it because of the sweet smell. Last year, when I was twelve, I got a very small bottle of scent that made me feel really grown up. This year, though, Mami asked me what I would like, so, as I am into reading French a lot these days, I asked her to get me a bible in French – so I could, like, compare it to the English. And she sent me this wonderful book with wooden covers. It's beautiful. So I am writing to her to say thank you for it.

'*Mami. Quelle merveilleuse surprise. Tu m'as donné la plus mignonne bible dans le monde. Je l'adore, et je vais le lire tous les jours. Merci mille fois...*'

Which is, like, saying it's a cool present. She always listens to what I'm interested in, what I really like, then gives me something much better than I could imagine.

A Wider World

Love is the Key

Bilal is sitting on a bench in a leafy churchyard with his head in his hands. Bilal is black. He is approached by a casually dressed man in his thirties of middle-eastern appearance (M-E guy).

M-E GUY   Hi mate. Got room for me?

BILAL   Oh. Yeah. Sorry. I... I'm going. The bench is yours.

Bilal gets up to move on.

M-E GUY   No, mate. Don't go away. Just budge up a bit.

BILAL   No. That's OK. I was just going anyway.

M-E GUY   Didn't look like you were. What're you doing here all on your own on a Sunday morning anyway?

BILAL   I'm on my own because I haven't got anyone here – in Britain.

M-E GUY   You a refugee? ... Sorry. Don't mean to pry. It's just I'm alone today, too.

BILAL   You a refugee, too, mate?

M-E GUY   Sort of. Certainly here – in this churchyard.

BILAL   How's that?

A middle-aged man and a woman walk by on their way to the church, totally ignoring the men on the bench as they pass.

M-E GUY   You tried to attend worship here, didn't you?

BILAL   Yes. How do you know?

M-E GUY   Saw the signs. You were rejected. Ignored you, did they? Pretended you weren't there?

BILAL   How'd you know that?

M-E GUY   Happens to me ... all the time.

BILAL   Happens to you? You've been in there ... more than once?

M-E GUY   Oh, I go in every week. But they don't notice me.

BILAL   Don't you ever want to give up? I mean being rejected once was going to be enough for me. Someone told me there's a

	church down the other end of town that might suit me better. They said it had interpreters.
M-E GUY	Doesn't sound to me like you need an interpreter.
BILAL	I was educated in English and Arabic, I don't expect people to speak my mother tongue.
M-E GUY	Africa?
BILAL	Sudan. My family are from the Nuba Mountains. They have fled to South Sudan and I learned I was on the police list. Had to get out. Hey. You're not one of them, are you? From the Sudanese secret police?

Bilal looks at him with concern and fear. Have the Sudanese secret police followed him to Britain?

BILAL	*Hal 'ant earabiat?*
M-E GUY	Am I Arabic? Sure I can speak and understand Arabic—
BILAL	Sorry. I mean … you're not a Muslim?
M-E GUY	In some ways. But no, I'm not a signed up Muslim.
BILAL	That's a relief. A Christian, then?
M-E GUY	Depends on what you think a Christian is.
BILAL	I think a Christian is – ought to be – someone who follows Jesus, accepts his love and seeks to love Him in return and love other people.
M-E GUY	'Love your God with all your heart, mind, soul and strength; and love others as you love yourself'?
BILAL	Exactly. *Thinking.* Hey… You're not a Jew?
M-E GUY	Depends on what you think a Jew is.
BILAL	Sounds like you are everything and nothing when it comes to religion.
M-E GUY	Oh, no. I'm not either 'everything' or 'nothing'. Let me explain. You say that being a Christian is all about love. Love is at the heart of it?
BILAL	Yeah. No one can be a Christian – a real Christian – without love.

M-E GUY	Right. So love is the key. 'God is Love'. If there is love in the heart of a Jew for God, then God must be there. Right?
BILAL	I suppose so.
M-E GUY	And if love is in the heart of Muslims when they pray to Allah, God has to be there. Right?
BILAL	I guess so. But Muslims have destroyed my home, persecuted my family, blown up my church in Khartoum and chased me out of Sudan.
M-E GUY	The people who have done that call themselves Muslims but is there love in their hearts?
BILAL	No way.
M-E GUY	Have you never met any kind, generous loving Muslims?
BILAL	Yes, of course. OK. I see what you're getting at. Love is the key but love is *central* to being a Christian. Christians preach love all the time. *Agape* love – self-giving love. The kind of love that Jesus has for us in dying for us on the cross.
M-E GUY	The kind of love that those people in the church behind us have shown you this morning?
BILAL	They didn't show any kind of love and welcome.
M-E GUY	But listen. They are singing songs of praise and love.

Strains of 'Love Divine' are heard from off-stage.

M-E GUY	I think you should go back and try to get in again.
BILAL	They'll only ignore me out again.
M-E GUY	You shouldn't give up. Take your love in there. Look I'll come with you. If they reject you, they'll reject me … again but one should never give up trying.
BILAL	Yeah but … being a refugee … I don't have much confidence. I just want someone, somewhere, to accept me.
M-E GUY	We'll do it together. I really want to get in there – and I reckon you understand love in the way they need to hear. They're frightened of you. In some ways you are bigger and stronger than them.

BILAL	You say all the right things. OK, I'll do it – if you come with me.

The two 'outsiders' leave the bench and approach the church. Lights go down, then up again.

Bilal returns to the bench accompanied by a friendly couple. He sits on the bench to get out his lunch. Couple wave goodbye. M-E Guy reappears.

M-E GUY	Hi Bilal. Budge up.
BILAL	Hello again. I got in! but where did you get to? When I got to the door I couldn't see you. You disappeared.
M-E GUY	I was with you, Bilal. You took me into the church in your heart. And you got me in for the first time in a few years! You have a job to do here, Bilal. What you have to do is love them until they learn the meaning of Love ... until they can sing love songs from the heart.
BILAL	I knew it, you're ...
M-E GUY	I am. Yes, I came to Bethlehem two thousand years ago. And I come again whenever anyone lets me in. I come into the hearts of all who love. I am with you always, Bilal, to the end of time... or until you decide to give up loving.
BILAL	I'll never do that, Lord.
M-E GUY	Teach them to love, Bilal. Love them and get them to open their hearts to me and let me in.

Sixty Thousand Girls

Abby who features in this story first appeared in the White Gates Adventures series. The story begins in Persham in the English midlands, the town from which the hero of the White Gates Adventures hails and the home of the 'kicking tree' which gives its name to the first book in the series.

As Ayeisha rounded the corner, a huge gust of wind almost took her off her feet.

'Where do you think you're going?' laughed her friend, Sarah. They clung to each other, their brown school blazers dragging them back as they battled forwards, shrieking with delight. They made it to Sarah's house. They had been coming to her place every maths homework day all that year. They always did their maths homework together, tackling each question separately, and only helping the other if one got stuck – which they rarely did. It was good teamwork. The wind had lifted the girls' spirits after the deadly business of the history lesson which ended the Year Nine school day. It wasn't the history that was the problem but the dull way Mr Banks intoned his way through his written notes – notes that had 'stood the test' (as he put it) of many years.

Sarah and Ayeisha had been best friends ever since they were six when Ayeisha first came to live in Persham in the English Midlands. She had been born in Somalia but her family had been granted asylum. Her father, Ishmael, had got a steady job as a bus driver, and her mother did part-time work in the electronics factory. They were soon able to move into a three-bedroomed housing association house in the same school catchment area as Sarah.

Sarah attended St Augustine's Church Sunday School, and Ayeisha the local mosque but her father approved of their friendship. There were too many who did nothing to worship God in Britain, and a religious family, albeit Christian, he believed was a good thing. Besides, having an English-born friend could be an advantage as his daughter grew.

Ishmael Bilal was a faithful and forward-thinking Muslim who loved his wife Miriam. He had run into trouble in Mogadishu when Al Shebab gained control there – he knew all about the extremists and their ways, and he did not like them. He refused to insist Ayeisha wear a veil-like Miriam – their faith was in Allah, he claimed, not tradition. Ayeisha could make up her own mind.

Ishmael passionately believed in girls' education; he wanted education for both his children. He was determined that both Ayeisha and her younger brother Mohammed should have opportunities denied to so many of his family in Somalia. Life in Britain was good to them.

But things were set to change.

At the same moment that his daughter was enjoying the battle with the wind on her way home from school, Ishmael was struggling through the town centre with his bus. The gale had caused a fall of tiles in the main street. After ten minutes he managed to negotiate the obstacle and was just accelerating in second gear when another roof shed its tiles – this time right in front of him. Debris crashed through the windscreen, hitting him in the face and neck. When they got to him, Ishmael was already dead.

The coroner issued a verdict of accidental death; he expressed his sadness at Mr Bilal's demise and extended sympathy to his family. The insurance company had called it an 'act of God' and, at his funeral only a day after his death, the imam called it the 'will of God'. Ayeisha found it hard to believe that God would do that.

Wanting to support Ayeisha, Sarah, her parents, the vicar and Abby his daughter – who was in Year 11 at Sarah's school – attended the funeral. There were few others there. The Muslim community was mostly Punjabi. Miriam felt very alone in England.

To lose a father at the age of fourteen was incredibly painful, and Ayeisha stayed away from school. The only person she wanted to see was Sarah.

Now without a father, Ayeisha and Mohammed, in the custom of their clan, became the responsibility of Ishmael's brother – as, indeed, Miriam was; as a woman, she did not have a say. The next adult male in line, Abdul, took his responsibilities seriously. Living in Mogadishu, he rather enjoyed having the status of dependents in the United Kingdom. Before she knew what was really going on, Ayeisha discovered that they were summoned to London to the house of a distant relative she had never met. She did not want to go, and her mother was distraught because she was all too aware of what might happen to them there. At fourteen, Ayeisha was of marriageable age, and Miriam was pretty sure that she would be sent back to Somalia where she would almost certainly suffer the torture of FGM. Ishmael had been a modern British Muslim but he had been alone in the family in his thinking. Miriam's family connections were all in Somalia, and would think it proper that Ayeisha be traditionally married as Miriam had been. She protested but her protests were ignored. She went to the imam, who simply shrugged his shoulders. He was a Pakistani, what could he do? These were the customs of her family, and they couldn't be gainsaid – they were the ones with the authority.

'Just tell them you don't want to go,' blurted Sarah when her friend told her what was happening.

'They know that. No girl wants to go. It's always like that.'

' But it's not right. You're fourteen. You've got a say.'

'No. In my community, it wouldn't make any difference if I were forty.'

'You're too young to be married – and what's all this about 'cutting'. What do you mean?'

'I'm not too young to be married in Somalia. Some girls marry even younger. No girl chooses when... or who to be married to.'

'What about your mum? Didn't she have a choice?'

'My father chose her.'

'Didn't she love him?'

'Yes. My father was a good man. He treated her well, and she grew to love him. My father said the Qur'an demands a man respect his wife. Yet he believed in girls' education and said any girl of his should not marry until she had finished her education. He believed the laws in Britain are good – that sharia law shouldn't apply in Britain, he said. Even in Somalia, he spoke out – that's why he and Mum had to come to the West.'

'And the 'cutting'?'

'Before you are married you must... you have to have your female parts cut. If I were in Somalia it would have already been done but my father would never have approved.'

'What... what do they do?'

'I don't want to talk about it. It's called Female Genital Mutilation in the West. In this country it is illegal – but it still happens. Anyway, people get sent back to Somalia for it... or whatever.'

'That's... that's disgusting. Ayeisha you have to stand up to this.'

'How? You don't understand—'

'Just don't go to London.'

'I won't have a choice. They'll come and take me. It won't be on a train or anything... Sarah, I'm scared.'

'We'll go to the police.'

'They won't do anything. Last year, Fatima... do you remember her? She was three years below us – second-year middle school.'

'Yes. She left. What happened to her?'

'She was taken back to... Africa, somewhere... I'm not sure exactly where. She went to the police. The police went and spoke to her parents but they still took her. The police don't understand. They don't want to get involved in things inside families – especially where race comes into it, too. Her father was a quiet man with a decent job—'

'But your father is dead.'

'That won't make any difference. Look, Sarah, it's happened before – the police won't touch it. It may be illegal to force me to leave to marry in this country – but no one ever does anything about it. It happens all the time.'

'I didn't realise—'

'Exactly. No one has any idea. No one will believe me.'

'I believe you.'

'Thanks, but what can you do about it?'

Sarah lay on her bed, thinking.

'I know. We'll run away.'

'Run away? But how? Where?'

'We'll take camping stuff. In a backpack... Look, if you're not here they can't take you anywhere, can they?'

'It won't work.'

'Of course it will. Let them come all the way from London. If they find you not here, they'll give up.'

'They won't give up. They'll keep looking for me. They're bound to come more than once.'

'We'll stay away for three weeks – and after that, you can stay at my house. They'll get the message soon enough. You watch; they'll give up and disappear. After all, your dad never contacted them, did he? Your relative is probably fed up with being given the responsibility of a family he doesn't know. We can stay away for three weeks. I have six hundred pounds in my account – that's one hundred pounds a week each. That's more than enough—'

'But, Sarah, you can't do that! What about your mum and dad? They wouldn't let you.'

'No. Perhaps not but they would understand.'

'Sarah! That's disrespectful.'

'Leave them to me. It'll be OK, I promise… Have you got a backpack?'

'No.'

'We'll have to get you one… I know, we'll ask Abby, the vicar's daughter, if we can borrow hers. She won't mind. I know she's got one – she used it to go to Soul Survivor last summer.'

'But they could come for me anytime.'

'OK. Cunning plan. You come to my house tomorrow. We'll have a sleepover for the weekend. We'll get everything we need on Saturday and get packed on Sunday afternoon. We'll leave the backpacks in my wardrobe. On Monday morning, we go to school as normal but instead of going in, we'll come straight back here, change and set off.'

'But where will we go?'

'To the seaside – the south coast. They have lots of places to camp there and there will be tourists from all over, we won't stand out. I've been there with Mum and Dad lots of times – and with the Scouts. That's how I know all about camping. We can both pass off as eighteen if we put on enough make-up. We'll pretend to be, like, students – geology students.'

'But we don't know anything about geology.'

'I do. I've read the local stuff and been to the museums. They call it the Jurassic Coast. Ayeisha, this is going to be cool, you'll love it.'

'Look at all those stars!' exclaimed Sarah, as they stood together on the shingle beach... 'They say that for every person on earth there's a hundred of them just in our Milky Way, without counting all the billions of other galaxies.'

'How'd you know that?' asked Ayeisha

'Don't know. Just heard it somewhere. I guess I could look it up on my smartphone.'

'I thought you said we should keep them turned off.'

'Yeah. Course... I just forgot. It's strange living in a world when you're not constantly online.'

'I like it... I think. It's peaceful,' said Ayeisha, wistfully, 'but I would hate just to disappear... forever.'

'But that's the point, Ayeisha. We're here to avoid anyone coming to take you away.'

'I miss my mum.'

'Look, Ayeisha, you've got to stay strong...'

'You said we were going to stay at a campsite.'

'Yeah. Sorry, I know. It hadn't occurred to me that they wouldn't be open in May. Look, tomorrow we'll find somewhere to put up our tent. We'll save money that way. We've got the sea... and we can go to the leisure centre and swim and shower there.'

'A hundred pounds sounds a lot but it isn't when you think about how much things cost.'

'Ayeisha. It'll be OK. Think about it... what choice do you have? Do you want to be whisked off to Somalia and be married off to some strange man?'

Ayeisha shuddered. 'What would I do without you, Sarah?'

'I don't know but you don't have to be without me. I'm not going anywhere. We've been best friends ever since you came to Persham... Do you remember Miss Wright in Year One? She used to go, 'You two are, like, tied together with some invisible cord. I daren't walk between you in case I trip up on it.''

'Yeah. And the following year Mr Adams made us sit on different tables so we didn't copy.'

'But he gave up after two weeks because he realised that we learned, like, better together. He went, 'Oh, Miss Bilal',' Sarah put on a 'Mr Adams' voice, 'if I let you and Miss Clough sit next to each other, will you promise me you won't cheat?'

The girls laughed as they reminisced under the stars until they fell into a fitful sleep to the sound of the gentle waves splashing and hissing back between the pebbles.

'This will make a great place,' stated Sarah, as she trod down the lush, young grass beside the river. They had left the main footpath and pushed their way through brambles, taking care not to slip into the river. The small patch of grass was hidden by a road bridge that passed high above them on one side and tall trees on the other. In front of them was the river with a high wall on the opposite bank.

'Perfect,' said Sarah emphatically. 'no one will ever know we're here. It can't be seen from the path.'

'What about the bridge?'

'No pedestrians allowed on it. And there is a weir upstream, so no one will come boating along here.'

The place was clean and sweet – it smelt of the new bright green grass mixed with the scents of young nettles, may blossom and a larger number of wildflowers than Ayeisha could ever remember in one spot. They stood still and listened. Apart from the noise of the traffic on the bridge, all they could hear was the sounds of nature – the call of a robin and a blackbird, who had given up his alarm call once the girls had stood still. A bumblebee buzzed by and settled on a yellow dandelion.

'OK… I'm hungry,' said Ayeisha.

'We'll have breakfast, then we'll put up the tent.' Sarah opened a bag that contained bread, apples and a plastic bottle of milk they had bought at the supermarket. She had calculated how much they could spend each day on food. The leisure centre was just up the road. Later they would check it out and find out how much it would cost to go for a swim. As they munched on the bread, they heard the sound of children.

'Don't worry,' said Sarah. 'They won't come this way. There's a school just over there. They'll be playing out.'

'We should be in school... I wonder what the teachers are saying in Persham?'

'Don't worry about it. I wrote it all out in the note I left my parents. I told them to say we won't be coming in.'

'Do you think they will have taken my letter round to my mum?'

'Of course. As soon as they found me missing yesterday, they would have opened my letter and found yours. They would have taken it straight round.'

'I think... I think my mum will understand.'

'My mum and dad will be cross but they'll get over it. I can just picture my dad: 'What the hell does she think she's playing at?!' And my mum saying, 'Calm down dear, she knows how to look after herself. She's had all that training with the Scouts and we've been camping every year since she was little. And she's done it for Ayeisha – you know Ayeisha just *had* to run away.'

They spent all that day and the next in their little campsite. Sarah was right, Ayeisha concluded, she did know how to look after herself. She checked their expenditure carefully, writing down everything they had spent. They kept to the simplest foods which may have been boring but were wholesome enough. The leisure centre was more expensive than they had bargained for – Sarah reckoned they could manage three or four visits in their time there.

On their fourth day, they walked back to the beach. They were enjoying a prolonged spell of May sunshine and decided it was certainly warm enough for a swim. The water was cold but wonderfully refreshing. They splashed and shouted in the surf. Ayeisha could only ever remember going to the seaside once before, and it was not like this. It was a place called Weston-super-Mare, she explained, where the beach was muddy and the waves tiny – not like this place with its shingle and surf.

They pulled themselves back up the steep beach and stretched out on their towels to dry off. There were few people about. The season hadn't really started. They had been there for perhaps fifteen minutes when they were approached by two boys carrying cans of beer.

'Hi, girls,' said one. 'You want some company?' He was rough looking but handsome in a rugged kind of way. He wore cut off jeans and a peaked cap. Nothing else. His mate, however, boasted a tatty white T-shirt with something like 'Surf City' on it; it was difficult to make out as the shirt was far too big for him.

Ayeisha sat up, alarmed.

'It's OK. I'm Pete. This here is Jed.'

'Hi,' said Sarah.

Invited or not, the boys sat on the shingle next to the girls. They explained they were preparing to go to college. They were on a gap year. (Ayeisha wished they weren't drinking. They smelled and belched but Sarah didn't seem to notice.) Sarah said it was the same for them. 'We're starting at university...' she lied, 'Bath. In the autumn.'

'Great. What're studying?'

'Geology.'

The lad didn't follow that up. Perhaps he didn't know much about it; he didn't seem to be very bright. Jed said nothing.

'Look, we're going to get some chips,' said Pete after a few minutes of inane talk. 'Interested?'

'Um... no,' replied Sarah as she thought to herself, *I could murder a bag of chips*. The smell had been making her salivate ever since they had got to the bay. 'We have no money for chips.'

'Nah. It's on us,' said Pete, 'innit Jed?' Jed nodded.

Sarah and Ayeisha tried not to show how hungry they were as they wolfed down large bags of fish and chips, and chased it with cokes. Ayeisha had been adamant that she did not want any beer. When they went to the public toilets, Sarah had whispered to her that it was OK. They were eighteen, weren't they? Muslims are not supposed to drink, Ayeisha had explained. And today was Friday of all days!

'You like being a Muslim?'

'I *am* a Muslim. God is good.'

Sarah smiled, 'It'll be alright. I can handle this. We got fed didn't we?'

Inshallah, Ayeisha thought to herself. There was a lot Sarah just did not understand. This whole escapade was such a game for her.

They returned to the beach but the quality of the conversation didn't improve. Sarah couldn't ascertain where the boys were headed, or what their gap year consisted of. Jed continued to say nothing but grunt – and belch. After a while, any interest Sarah might have had in Pete completely died. Ayeisha was uncomfortable. Sarah decided they had been on the beach long enough.

Then the trouble started. The beer-drinking had continued on and off for the past three hours and the lads were clearly affected. Sarah said it was time to find some shade, and Pete suggested they head along the path that led up the cliff.

'There's a place we could go up there. When you get to the top there's bushes and stuff. We could go in there and, you know...' he chortled, 'we'd have no one to bother us.'

'No. We have to go home... I mean back to our people,' said Sarah hurriedly.

'Oh, go on,' said Pete laying his hand on Sarah's bottom. 'Don't you fancy a bit of—'

'No!' she said, knocking him away. She told herself, *I said I could handle this and I will.* 'Thanks for the chips but we really should be going now. Come on Ayeisha.'

They strode up the beach and around the harbour. The boys followed. It was evident that they were not going to be shaken off; if they had had any inhibitions they had long since dissolved in alcohol. Sarah tugged Ayeisha into a bus queue just as a double-decker bus drew up. They followed the line of people and Sarah pulled out her wallet.

'Town,' she asked the driver. 'Two.' They took their tickets and headed up the stairs.

The fare was more than Sarah had anticipated but there was nothing for it. The lads hesitated but at the last minute decided to get on too. The driver was, however, alert to what was going on.

'No. Off my bus,' he barked. 'No one with cans on this bus.'

'We'll leave them.'

'You're drunk. Off!'

Pete and Jed, lost for a reply, obeyed. As the bus swung around the corner, the girls saw the boys crossing the road back to the harbour – still with their beer in hand.'

'That was expensive,' said Ayeisha.

'I know. But we've got rid of them.' Sarah laughed, 'Goes to show they're right what they say: 'There's no such thing as a free lunch.' Then Ayeisha laughed too.

'I'm glad you didn't drink any beer,' she said.

'So am I. You know what, Ayeisha, we're a good team.' Ayeisha smiled.

'If I got pregnant, my relatives would wash their hands of me.'

'What! Have sex with *them*? Have a baby with that trash? You must be kidding me.'

'Some girls have done worse,' sighed Ayeisha. ' but it might not work – they could kill me for it.'

'Explain.'

'If a girl brings shame on her family, like even having a boyfriend, her relatives can kill them – an honour killing.'

'They don't!... do they?'

Ayeisha nodded. Sarah had so much to learn.

Sarah and Ayeisha's three weeks suddenly became one-and-a-half. One day they returned to their tent to discover that not only had they been discovered but they had also been robbed. All their stuff had been taken – the tent, the little cooking stove, their small stash of food, as well as the rest of the cash so carefully hoarded. Sarah had hidden it in her sleeping bag – but, of course, that was gone too. All the girls were left with was a collection of clothes, mostly unwashed, scattered in the undergrowth.

'So what now?' asked Ayeisha calmly. Sarah struggled to hold back the tears. 'Time to break radio silence,' she sighed.

To say that Sarah had underestimated the distress she had left her parents in was putting it mildly. Hadn't her note explained everything? Didn't they know that she was quite capable of looking after herself? Why did they have to get half the police force out looking for them? The worst was that they were too upset to get cross with her. Her mum couldn't stop cuddling her.

Ayeisha's mum was much calmer. She trusted Sarah and she understood and it was comforting to have Sarah's mum and dad to share the waiting with. She herself had been a refugee and knew that sometimes you have to flee.

It was the policewoman who was the most vehement in her criticism of what they had done. Sarah was made to promise never to do the same thing again. She promised she wouldn't; she had misjudged the impact it would have on her family. Yet she didn't regret trying to protect her friend; she hoped that people had listened to the reasons. They hadn't run away – she had merely taken Ayeisha away for a few days to get her away from home.

Abby came round.

'I do understand why you did it, Sarah,' she said.

'Thanks. I'm glad someone gets it,' sighed Sarah.

'They do. But everyone was so worried about you. If you'd kept your phone on that would have helped.'

'Yeah. And Dad would have shown up the next day and brought us home.'

'What you did was dangerous, Sarah.'

' We were managing very well... until some idiot robbed us.'

'That's the point, isn't it? Suppose that 'idiot' turned up while you were in your tent asleep?'

'He wouldn't have nicked our stuff.'

'Wouldn't he? I don't want to frighten you but the world isn't all as good as the people you know. Promise me you won't do it again.'

'Yeah. Don't worry, Abby. I won't upset people like that again.'

Sarah and Ayeisha sat outside the head's office waiting to be called in. They spotted Abby's blonde hair. Seeing them there, Abby came across.

'Hi. You look lined up for a rollicking?'

'Yeah.'

'Good luck.'

'Thanks. We'll need it.'

'Sarah, Ayeisha,' called the head's secretary through the door. 'Mr Whitecastle will see you now.'

'Thanks,' answered Sarah, meekly. She felt sick and about to wet herself. *Don't be scared*, she told herself, *we did the right thing... He might be kind and understand. Be brave*. However, Mr Samuel Whitecastle's reputation was not one of sympathy. And there wasn't any. Any hope that the head would understand the girls was quickly dissipated.

'What, if I may ask, were you two doing by disappearing for a whole fortnight? In May, of all times, when examinations demand the absence of any disruption to the school.'

'Ayeisha was scared of being taken to London,' replied Sarah.

'Let Ayeisha speak for herself,' demanded Mr Whitecastle. Ayeisha sat mute. 'Well, haven't you got a tongue, girl?'

'I was frightened, sir.'

'If that was the case, you should have come to me. Absconding doesn't solve the problem.'

'Would you have stopped them taking Ayeisha away?' asked Sarah, innocently. She didn't mean to be rude.

Mr Whitecastle stood up and looked Sarah straight in the eyes. He rose above her, ferocious. Sarah remembered someone saying about what a tiger was supposed to do just before it struck. She decided not to cower but keep her eyes fixed on his. 'Sarah Clough,' he spat, 'I am shocked that you, who have made such an excellent start in this school, should turn out to be so disrespectful and arrogant, and to challenge not only me and the staff of this school but your parents, your community, the police and a good many other people. You have let us *all* down... I put it to you, Miss Clough, that this... this escapade was *your* idea, and that *you* led this fellow student to share your prank... Are you aware of the implications of this?'

'Ayeisha needed to get away—'

'Nonsense! We live in a civilised country governed by law, Miss Clough, or hadn't you realised that? What have you achieved by this absconding, eh?'

Sarah sat thinking how best to explain to this man. He just didn't get it. He didn't want to get it. All of a sudden she began to realise the full reason why Ayeisha had said it was hopeless. She was totally frustrated. She didn't know how to answer him. She was both shocked and intimidated.

'You may well sit there silent. I'll tell you. Nothing. This will be on your record forever. You will never be able to expunge it. And you have dragged this school down with you. I and the governors are *very*, and I mean *very*, disappointed in you.'

'But—'

'Silence girl! The question remains of how we are to punish you. You do realise that expulsion is not out of the question? If it were left to me, I would suspend you but the staff and the governors feel that on this occasion, this *exceptional* occasion, you are to be given a severe warning and put on notice. You will report to your head of year every morning at 8.30 am sharp, and you will serve five weeks detention, during which time you will catch up on all that you have missed while you were away... Do you understand?' Ayeisha nodded, Sarah sat - defiant. This just wasn't fair! 'Do you understand, Miss Clough?'

'Yes.'

'Yes, what?'

'Yes, sir.'

'Now go straight to your lessons. Don't forget, Miss Clough, I'll be watching you!'

Sarah had entered the office nervous, she departed furious. She was amazed at how angry she felt.

'That was completely out of order,' said Ayeisha. 'He and my uncle are the same.'

'How so?'

'Puffed up male despots but they don't realise it... I don't mind the detention. I'll be safer in school.'

'I don't expect they'll still want you to go to London now. Thank God all that's blown over.'

'Maybe...'

'What! Just disappeared?' Abby stood open-mouthed. It was less than one week after they had got home.

'Yeah', replied Sarah with a sigh and a tear. 'Yesterday. The neighbours said that a big black car drew up. Two men in Muslim dress got out and went into the Bilal's flat. There was some shouting and the neighbours got anxious. Some of them went around to see what was happening but they met Mrs Bilal, Ayeisha and Mohammed at the door with suitcases. Mrs Bilal curtly explained that they were leaving. Apparently, Ayeisha was wrapped in a black cloth. They got into the car and it drove off.'

'Where were they going?' asked Abby.

'They didn't say but I expect it's London somewhere. Ayeisha's relative lives there.'

'What about Social Services? Have you reported it?'

'Mum did. They said this is not uncommon. They would contact their department in London and ask them to look out for them... but they don't hold out much hope.' Sarah began to sob. She had dared to think they had done enough.

'What about the police? Surely the police could find the relative.'

'Mum rang but they said there was no crime. Mrs Bilal was not abducted or anything. She left voluntarily.'

'But it wasn't voluntarily. She didn't want to go. She had no choice!'

'But she didn't contact the police – didn't put up a fight. She packed a suitcase.'

'It's wrong! What if, what if they... they 'cut' her? I know it's been illegal in Britain for thirty years but no one's ever been found guilty of doing it. They do what they want... They'll mutilate her and send her to Somalia to be married... She'd rather die, I know she would.' Sarah gasped. The thought of it was terrifying. If it were her, she would commit suicide. Perhaps Ayeisha... Oh, God...

'I think you should tell the police that. If you think her relative is planning to mutilate her, then, surely, they'll have to act.'

'I'm not best friends with the police – not since we ran away. They told me wasting police time is a chargeable offence.'

'We'll tell my dad. He'll contact them.'

Abby sat in silence for all of a minute, her head bowed and her blonde hair obscuring her features. Sarah felt defeated – even Abby seemed stumped, but then Abby straightened up decisively.

'We must tell the world!' she exclaimed.

'How do you mean?'

'Write your story. Write her story. Facebook, TikTok, Twitter. Instagram – everywhere. We'll start a blog. Send stuff to the papers, start a petition...'

'By the time I've finished doing all that, it'll be too late. It's too late already.'

'Maybe for Ayeisha but not for the next girl, and the one after that. Let's get to work. You know I'm the editor of the school student rag mag?'

'No! Wow!'

'Yes. We'll get something in the next issue.'

'But Mr Whitecastle would—'

'Don't worry about that. I'll handle him.'

'But... you know, all that stuff about the school record. He wouldn't want anything written about Ayeisha, or me.'

'And that's the problem, isn't it?' said Abby.

'What?'

'It's just one big cover-up. Everyone wants to wash their hands of it. The cops won't act because it's domestic and race. Social Services say it's not in their area, and the Church will say it's a Muslim issue, while the imam is, himself, intimidated along with the rest of the community.'

'How many girls are in Ayeisha's situation do you think?'

'In Britain? Don't know. But across the world, hundreds of thousands – millions even.' Abby took out her smartphone and began tapping. 'Wow! If you google 'FGM' you get loads of stuff...somebody's making a fuss about it... Woah, 'Forward UK' says that probably one hundred and thirty million women worldwide have had it done. And one hundred and thirty-seven thousand women and girls in the UK are living with the consequences – and *sixty thousand* girls here in the UK are at risk!'

'Sixty thousand! That's ridiculous. And you say there are already people complaining. So what's the point in me writing anything? We – you and I, what can we do?'

'So we give up? I don't think so. Look, even if we work for ten years – twenty years – and save one girl it would be worth it, wouldn't it? Get writing, Sarah… '

The big black car had headed for the motorway. There were two men, both Somalis. They said they were not relatives, just people acting for them. Ayeisha had tried to call Sarah as soon as they had arrived at the house – but one of the men spotted her phone and took it from her. Without it she felt almost naked and, despite her mum and brother, she had never felt so alone. She longed for her dad.

Before the car reached the motorway, the driver pulled into a garage and began to fill the tank. Desperate to try anything, Ayeisha said she needed to go to the loo. She called upon her dad and asked him to seek Allah's help. The second man didn't much care for the idea but it was going to be some hours before they next intended to stop. He consented reluctantly and walked her over towards the shop. Ayeisha went through the door with the word 'toilet' on it. To her surprise, the door opened onto a short corridor with a second door to the toilet on her left – in front was a back door that led outside. She didn't need a second invitation. She had run away once, she could do it again. Discarding her black robe, she crossed the yard and leapt over the back gate. She found herself in a lane that led both ways. She elected to turn right – the end of the lane was nearer in that direction. Emerging from the lane she turned left along a road that led her into an estate of houses. She dreaded the black car coming down the road, so dived off into a churchyard. Beyond the churchyard was an open field. She didn't want to be caught in the open countryside. The great wooden door of the church, however, stood open. It was an old church – there would be lots of nooks and crannies to hide in.

Inside it was comfortably dingy. The far aisle was particularly gloomy. She heard a sound, and realised that there must be someone in the church somewhere – a light streamed from a tiny door towards the front. Ayeisha made for the far aisle. Where could she hide? She saw a side altar with a colourful cover right down to the floor on all sides. She touched it – it was hanging loose. Ayeisha prayed and lifted the heavy cloth; the back was not covered but you could not see that unless you went right around the altar. Ayeisha heard footsteps coming up the church path. Panicking, she dived behind the altar and underneath it. She tried to control her breathing and keep as still as she could.

A light went on in the side chapel – but Ayeisha was completely hidden. She heard someone coming in and sitting down in front of the altar. She was trapped. More footsteps, and then a man spoke: 'Good morning Mrs Smith. Mrs Taylor coming?'

'Yes, vicar... Ah, here she is.'

Ayeisha heard Mrs Taylor greet them and take a seat somewhere next to Mrs Smith. A third person crept into the church and joined them but the gentle silence was broken by pounding feet.

'Good morning, gentlemen,' said the vicar. 'You are just in time for our mid-week communion service. We're over in the south aisle.'

'Er. No!' wheezed one of Ayeisha's captors. 'We're looking for a girl.'

'A girl? Well you see there is no girl here. What kind of girl?'

'She's fourteen. Er ... a black girl.'

'Ah. No, we haven't seen anyone of that description.' The three ladies murmured they hadn't either. 'Is she lost?'

'Er... yes.'

'Give me your phone number and I will tell you if she comes to light.'

'No. That's OK.'

'She can't be far,' said the other in a language Ayeisha understood but the vicar didn't. 'Come on Ali, we're wasting our time here.'

'We'll pray for her... and you,' said the vicar.

Ayeisha froze. The men went. Two minutes passed. It felt like an hour. Finally, the vicar padded back to the chapel, approached the altar and put something on it. He read some prayers. Two Bible readings followed and the vicar commented on them. He said something about God being ever-present and all-knowing. It occurred to Ayeisha that only she and God knew where she was at this moment. She hoped her mum would not be too worried; she had been amazed at how little she had got into trouble with her mum the last time she ran away. Not like Sarah who had got into really deep water.

Ayeisha was getting cramp – but she daren't move.

More prayers, and then the vicar came right up to the altar... and stepped around the back. He couldn't help but notice his unseen guest. Remarkably he said nothing. He stood up to the altar and began a prayer about the Last Supper of Jesus. Now she was discovered, but it was evident this man was not going to give her away – yet.

The service over, the vicar and congregation went to the great oak door of the church but the vicar asked Mrs Smith to stay – there was something he needed to talk to her about. He spoke in an undertone. They came back to the side-chapel. 'You can come out now, Miss,' said the vicar. 'The service is over, and the door is shut.' Ayeisha dragged herself out, guiltily, from her hiding place, and onto her feet. 'Are you going to tell us what this is all about?'

The man reminded her of Sarah's friend, Abby's father. He was clad in white robes with a green scarf.

'I'm... sorry... I ran away. I had to.'

To her absolute delight, Mrs Smith, who turned out to be about her mother's age, knew a lot about Somalia.

'Call the police, vicar. What has happened to this child is illegal.'

'But,' protested Ayeisha, 'the police will take me home... I can't go home. There's no one there and they'll only find me again.'

'The police,' said Mrs Smith, 'will take you into care. And if your relative makes any move to send you to Somalia, he will be arrested. It was on the news only last week. The government are getting tough on this. In actual fact, I think we are obliged by law to report it if we think any girl is in danger of FGM. If the police, here, don't do the right thing, I shall remind them of their responsibilities. And I'm sure the vicar will do the same.'

The vicar nodded. 'Indeed!' he said.

A week later, Ayeisha was back in Persham staying at Sarah's house. Sarah and their other friends were under strict orders never to leave Ayeisha on her own. Not that that was very different from how it had always been.

The London police were looking for her mother and brother with the cooperation of the local imams that served the Somali community.

Ten days later, their captors simply released them onto the street. They had become too hot.

After that, Ayeisha took more control. The local Muslims respected her for her stand, and she grew in confidence.

And somehow, at the school, the detention order placed on her and Sarah kind of vanished, and Mr Whitecastle was all sweetness and light. Perhaps he had learned as much as anybody. Remarkably, when the girls got their reports at the end of July, there was no mention of any of the events. *So much for it being on record forever,* thought Sarah.

But no one was ever really the same. Abby rejoiced in Ayeisha's rescue – but did not give up campaigning. True to her promise, she published Sarah's piece in the next school rag mag. If only they could save them all! All sixty-thousand girls at risk!

Peace

War-torn, worn world yearns, searches for Peace!
Peace, peace! Stop the warring, killing, let the maiming cease!
Peace! Paix! Shalom! Salaam! Frieden! Paz! Herping....
A trillion lips – screaming, summoning, murmuring, mouthing.
Call a cease-fire, sign a truce, turn your efforts to global warming.

We have our reward, the cost of conflict: the carpets of crosses and crescents
in poppy-strewn graveyards, blood-stained grass and sand. We stand in evil's
presence.
The mass burials of the ethnically cleansed, unspeakable piles of corpses extend
into the minds of the young – their lovely lives powerless to defend.
Humanity stinks – violence, lies, vicious ugliness; why prevaricate? Why pretend?

Dear Lord, have mercy!... make it all to cease!
Requiescat in pace – rest ... rest ... rest in peace.

Then we have it – proclaimed and promised. We rejoice but it's all deceit,
Empty words, false hopes, fleeting will-o'-wisp. Again we weep.
Weary warriors sent back to battle. Release the rockets, deploy the fleet,
lay land mines to maim, and kill the kids with unspeakable chemical ...
Leaders preach lies, talk up hatred and fear, then build another wall.

Dear Lord, have mercy!... make it all to cease!
Requiescat in pace – rest ... rest ... rest in peace.

Peace! Whispered in the smoke-laden wind;
Passion-pursued, patiently planned, hopes firmly pinned,

Dared dreams breathed ... then betrayed, slipping from our hands
on the blood-soaked battlegrounds of self-appointed bands;
and dissolving, dissipating ... front lines redrawn, barracks re-manned.

Negotiate! Talks about talks in high-style hotels;
Blood-seeking belligerence bared in bars and board room.
Summits scheme and slice, and leaders lounge in luxury;
while militias, unpaid and unfed, loot and kill, and children go hungry
or die at sea as exploited illegal immigrants, forced to flee.

'Weapons win wars,' greedy arms dealers say,
'while words are weakness and compromise brings shame.
Don't be fooled by doves and pleas. We guarantee to kill and maim.
Buy from us and we'll supply. We have ways to help you pay.
Put in your order today, right away – you know it's the only way.'

Unforgiving and unforgiven retain and recall ...
Resentments fester, ignorance, intolerance and revenge is all,
communities collapse and collide:
families feud, jealousies divide,
and rivals refuse to heed God's call.

Dear Lord, have mercy!... make it all to cease!
Requiescat in pace – rest ... rest ... rest in peace.

Where, then, is the hope? Is there ever peace before the grave?
In truth...? In truth, there can be no true peace while souls live enslaved,
and selfish self-seeking reigns – all mercy waived.
In a world where life's juice gels and love leaks, leaves

For hate, hunger and hopelessness ... Mangled hearts no longer believe.

The silent battleground: each broken soul, bared, battered:
hearts hurt forever rehearsing fire-fights fought, sleepless, shattered
reliving longings for loves long since lost. Lingering
memories of once wonderful scent-laden sunrise, birds singing
and sweethearts living heaven's peace – love-soaked revelling.

Dear Lord, have mercy!... make it all to cease!
Requiescat in pace – rest ... rest ... rest in peace.

Yet take heart, O soul. For hope remains firmly underpinned.
Love dwells yet, hidden yes, yet strong, undefeated, undimmed
breaking through heats of hatred, weeds of wickedness strimmed.
Raw, red anger runs dry and wet tears reveal its cost,
Love bubbles up from depths unknown – unseen depths where love's never lost.

Immersed in realities beyond maths' reach
- spirit infusing fermion and quark ... each
unseen force forging, forming, composing God's creation rhyme ...
Each hungry heart, hear a voice from outside space and time.
'My daughter you are loved, my son you are mine.'

Inside and out, light in darkness, life in death,
hope dispelling despair, love, refreshing heaven's breath.
Love heals, making whole and holy, building nature's bond;
Pouring peace-power within, beneath, between, beyond.
Restoring abused, damaged, wounded and wronged.

Sister, brother, former foe and friend: fellow travellers now;
all pursuance of politics, history and hate fade before God's vow,
'Write this for these words are trustworthy and true,' Not knowing how
all will become one in him, made new, his Holy Spirit overshadowing
ushering in God's deep peace:

a 'peace that passes all understanding'.

Heart to Heart

The party, in two vehicles, made their way up the bumpy road that led to the refugee camp on the outskirts of the city. It had taken three days to obtain permission to visit the people living under white plastic sheets bearing the pale blue United Nations IOM logo. The sheets adjoined one another in close rows, like little blue-and-white pigeon holes close to the ground. It was the rainy season and the narrow unmade tracks between the rows had turned into thick mud lined with puddles, which spread inside the shelters.

Hundreds of people, dressed in a variety of tattered and dirty clothes, were sitting, standing or squatting, staring at us, the visitors, in the four-wheel-drive cars as we ploughed on towards a series of central buildings – large hangar-like places with concrete floors. Here we were to meet a group of representatives from the churches – pastors and Mothers' Union leaders.

As a rule, despite the usual poverty of the country, the people were mostly clean and their eyes bright. These people, by contrast, were clearly malnourished – even the young mothers, who could not have been out of their twenties, looked old and worn. They were only a few miles from their homes in the city where they once had had employment – some teachers, some business owners, some neatly dressed secretaries and office workers with polished shoes.

When the inter-tribal conflict began they had fled – with just cause. Bands of young men with pangas and other tools turned into weapons – even the occasional AK47 – had begun killing and maiming members of their rival tribes indiscriminately. No one intervened. The national crisis had begun between rival tribes within the army and across the country civil war was taking hold. These people were on the losing side.

The UN had sent a peace-keeping force and set up Protection of Civilian (POC) camps to which the persecuted flocked in their thousands. To keep people safe, the boundaries were kept to a minimum – as always the UN were understaffed and the foreign aid not coming in as promised. It was a logistical nightmare and dangerous.

All over the world, when children are together, they are usually noisy – schoolyards echo with their calls and excited children play. Everywhere I've been, in desert and jungle as well as urban sprawl, the children seem to be everywhere making the most of things and coming out to see what all the fuss was about when a foreigner like me appears. Yet, despite there being many children here in this camp, they sat or stood silently and sullenly. Not one of them was playing – not that they had any toys to play with, of course. It was unreal, all wrong – the spirit of childhood had completely vanished. There were no separate groups of teenagers – they just blended into the adults. Education stops here at Year 4 – and it isn't every child who gets a chance to attend school in this country let alone inside a POC camp in a time of civil war.

And older people? Come to think of it, I don't remember seeing anyone beyond middle age, here.

Inside the building, dusty plastic chairs were procured for the visitors. We sat in a wide circle with nothing but the concrete floor between us. One of the local pastors got to his feet and gave a long speech of welcome in his tribal language, which was translated into English by a young man who stood next to him. This was followed by an equally long speech by a bishop of our party expressing his thanks at the welcome we had received and how important it was that in Christ there are no tribes or divisions and we had come to show that peace and reconciliation were at the heart of God.

I was reminded of the courage of the church leadership which was so outspoken against factions and corruption and violence of every kind. This is a brave thing to do in a country where people who oppose the powerful can find themselves taken in hand and interrogated in the notorious Blue House from which they do not return unscathed, if at all.

The church is also outspoken against the common practice of polygamy and promotes gender equality. Women were represented in and around our circle in equal numbers to the men. Some of the younger ones came round with boxes containing bottles of cold water and sodas. This was a gift of enormous generosity. Cold sodas are common outside the camp but here no one drank such luxuries but they had been obtained by some means – probably at the expense of food for their families.

The girls were followed by two women carrying a bowl of water with which to wash their guests. This would have been a normal greeting for honoured guests beyond the fence where soap would always have been produced, too; here there was no bar of soap. With their own hands, they set about washing our feet, hands and faces. More women followed up with towels. The honour which they showed us was unequalled – I have rarely been treated so much like a prince. Water – precious water – was all these people could give, and they gave it.

When people have almost nothing, it is not only food, clothing and dignity they lack – but also the ability to give; the freedom to be generous is at the heart of what it means to be human. If I have ever doubted that in the past, after this experience I never will.

Each of the party was invited in turn to say where they came from. The places and institutions we represented were of the utmost importance – it declared that the residents were not completely ignored by the outside world, not unwanted and forgotten about, buried alive in some kind of human refuse dump. I felt small and completely inadequate. These people were almost worshipping us. Very few people from beyond the gates – especially from outside the country – had deigned to come near the camp.

More speeches followed. One of the young mothers spoke of her distress and pain. We heard her stories and her anger at broken promises. She was calmed by an older woman. *Yet*, I thought, *why should she accept what was happening to her and her babies without complaining?* What could we say? Later, back in my own country, I was warned that I had to temper my outrage – sit on my hands – literally – to prevent me from going off on a rant. People do not like to hear about things that make them feel guilty of being comfortable.

The ability to pray together with these people and to acknowledge our oneness in God was never so important. We didn't celebrate Holy Communion with bread and wine but the communion in the Spirit was just as powerful.

The visit was all too short. We were soon led back to our vehicles, the men shook our hands warmly, and the women clustered around the female visitors, touching, stroking, and smiling. One lady invited one of them to stay.

'Will you not stay with us one night – come and eat with us – meet the children? We have not much but you are welcome to what we have.'

The visitor knew that they would have gladly gone without food for a whole day to have the privilege of someone from the outside staying with them – a little chink of hope, light from the other side of the fence but, of course, it was not possible. None of us had permission to remain. We were soon being ushered out of the camp, our passports checked and our names ticked off the list by the camp guards – UN guards whose role it was to protect the refugees.

Outside, we sped down the open road lined at first by empty bush, then wooden houses, tin-roofed shops and laughing children in school uniforms – we were free! We were on our way back to our lodgings for an evening meal.
The camp residents may be forgotten or rejected and neglected by most of the wider world but not by God. As we, the visitors, retreat, it is God who stays.

That Is It!

'That is it!' for the South Sudanese means, 'That is where the truth lies.' It does not mean, 'That is the end,' as it so often does in the West where, for many, hope has died long ago.

Juba.
City of birdsong,
laughing children,
people greeting.

Chugging generators,
Bodabodas' buzzing,
throbbing truck traffic,
aeroplanes roaring on runways.

That is it!

Choirs singing,
People praising,
Soloist with top notes off-key,
amplified keyboard commanding the air.

Trill of evening crickets,
Mosquitoes' high-pitched hum,
Men mingling around an after-meal fire,
Children protesting, resisting their sleeping nets.

That is it!

Desperate dogs baying without end,
Cockerels crowing at one a.m.
Bats calling as they circle the neems[2],
All-night vigil with Spirit-led preaching from two to four.

Muezzins waking the faithful at five,
Morning chorus greeting the sun,
Women sweeping with swish of broom,
Children calling as they dress for school.

That is it!

Student-filled streets – uniforms blue, yellow and green
Immaculate office workers in suits African style,
Women selling tea, chairs circled in hope;
men manning tin-roofed shops – bread, soap, and sodas in fridges without power.

Girls cooking on charcoal – asida[3], okra, rice, beans and greens,
Men with coal-filled smoothing irons.
Women washing, carrying bundles and pots on their heads.
All beneath the trees –
moringa, mango, guava, frangipani white-yellow and ruby red.

For two years and more this was home for me –
the beginning of a love story ...

That is it!
A love story.

Yet this is not yet Paradise, Eden – not yet.
Gunshot,
violence,
crime and corruption sully the beauty.
Children tortured,
girls raped,
men shot,
families fled
– separation,
misery,
pain.
Not one unscathed.

Fragmented thinking,
short term plans too small;
A people divided,
fractured –
distrusting,
Poverty rife –
tractors rusting,
Wasted opportunities,
pillaged potential –
symbolised in rubbish-laden streets.

That is it!

Centuries of exploitation –
slavery, food and now oil;
War the theme –
wars of power and control.
Failed governments,
overseas aid melting into oblivion
– someone has it somewhere, who knows where but not the devoted teacher or his
class.
Not the mother labouring to bring up her family without complaint;
Not the student seeking to fulfil her potential and giving thanks for the gift of a
pen;
Not the pastor working without pay;
Not the farmer planting, labouring to harvest – praying for rain and that the
soldiers don't come.

And that is it!
And yet ... And yet ...

A city where death gives way to life,
mourning to hope.
A city of giving and giving again ...
of starting and starting once more;
A city in which, 'Don't worry – God has tomorrow in His hands,' is lived for real.
A city of people who never give up –
where goodness, faithfulness, thankfulness and beauty heal!

That is it – a city of never giving in,
never letting darkness win –
working for each new today.
One day,
my friend,
one day ...

That is it!
That is it!

1. 'bodaboda'. A motorbike taxi.

2. 'neems'. The neem tree, originally from South Asia is common in urban South Sudan.

3. 'asida'. Or, in Swahili, 'ugali' is a stiff porridge of maize or another carbohydrate, a staple favoured by South Sudanese and East Africa in general.

The Bridge

This story first appeared at an event in the Bristol Festival of Literature in October 2019 and was subsequently broadcast on BBC Radio Bristol.

Tishala clambered up the steps of the footbridge that spanned the M32 from St Werburgh's to Easton. It was warm for September and the steel felt hot to touch as the teenager leant on the rail and watched the traffic speeding out of the city. She often did this. Sometimes she would pick out a car or a lorry and follow it until it disappeared from view and then she would imagine it zooming off to the M4 and beyond – London, perhaps, or South Wales, or even a port where it would roll aboard a boat. And then she would give thanks that she didn't have to go anywhere anymore – she was putting down roots in Bristol.

They had not been in the flat above the shop in Easton very long – less than six months. It had not been easy getting used to being away from South Sudan where Tish had belonged for her fourteen years until now.

Her story was simple. She had been doing well in Juba Diocesan Model Secondary School as her father's little business had grown. Its success, however, was too much for the criminals taking advantage of the lack of law and order to resist targetting it. Tish had returned home to find a blackened burnt shell, a distraught father and a dead mother. Their little business had been attacked and torched and her mother had died in the blaze.

Tish's father, although being South Sudanese, had been born in Britain. He sold what possessions he still had, gathered up his precious daughter and headed for the airport with just one suitcase. A couple they met on the plane had taken pity on them and had brought them to their home in Bristol because they had nowhere to go and no money.

Tishala had joined a local secondary school. The schoolwork was not so difficult; getting settled among young people who lacked motivation and who hated school was harder. This phenomenon was new to her; in Juba, a place at a secondary school was a precious thing – a privilege and an honour but here in Bristol, she had been automatically enrolled! Tish smiled to herself as she leaned against the rail; there were opportunities in this city.

It was then that she spotted Dean Jameson climbing the stairs. He could be nasty; he did not like swats and he tormented her whenever he got the chance. Tish fled to the Easton end of the bridge, down past the primary school and into Junction 3 library. She liked the library. So many books! And Dean wouldn't follow her there.

Sitting at a table, Tish reflected that perhaps she wouldn't have to cope with Dean and his cronies for much longer. That morning a posh looking letter had arrived from a boarding school in Somerset. Her enterprising father had applied for a bursary explaining their situation and this was the reply. Tishala had been invited to visit and if they liked the look of her and she of them, she could spend three days at the school as a trial. Her father was delighted for her but Tish was not so sure; she knew he would be bereft without her. Nevertheless, he would be cross if she didn't at least check it out.

Two weeks later, Tishala found herself surrounded by friendly girls – none of them black like her but nevertheless claiming her as one of their own. None of them knew much about South Sudan and didn't seem to want to. They were much brighter than most of those in her Bristol school and, since their parents were paying large fees for them to be there, they were obliged to be motivated.

'Well, Tishala, you have acquitted yourself well on your first day,' pronounced a neat woman introducing herself as head of year. 'You are clearly academically able if a little behind but with the right kind of remedial attention and some hard work from you, I'm sure we can get you up to speed before you sit your GCSEs. We'll consider your application and let you know.'

'Thank you, Miss.' Tish smiled. Her father would be pleased.

Back in Bristol, however, her father had some news to share. An email had arrived from his wife's brother in Juba. Things there seemed to have improved and food was not so much of a problem and he and his family had been discussing their situation. If Tish wanted to travel back to South Sudan, they would accommodate her and feed her with her cousins and, if her father could pay for her school fees, get her back into her old school.

Tish's heart leapt. Back with her friends! Back where she had grown up. Back home where she felt she belonged. No winter, and no Dean Jameson! She liked her mother's family. In truth, she had had no time to grieve – they had left as soon as was decent following her mother's funeral. It was a tempting prospect.

In her mind's eye, she took the bus from the Juba suburb of Munuki to Hai Mission and walked through the school gates. Then she was back, chatting in Juba Arabic with her friends. It was clear that the staff were pleased to see her, too; they were proud of her. She felt good in the heat and the dust and the city smells – even the buzz of the mosquitoes in her ear. Home! but with no mother and no father – in this place, she would really notice their absence.

That night, in her bed with the window shut against a cold autumn wind, she imagined herself back under a mosquito net in Juba. The noises of the darkness were different here. The continual barking of the neighbour's dog was fine, if annoying, and the sound of a noisy all-night vigil from the church was comforting; it was the gunfire that unnerved her. The violence that had resulted in her mother's death all of a sudden came flooding back. The dark terrors that lived in her heart just below the surface had not gone away. In her dream, she called to her father but he was not there!

Tishala awoke in a pool of sweat.

Still shaking, she stumbled to the bathroom and breathed a sigh of relief when she heard her father's gentle snoring coming from his room.

The next day was Saturday. No school.

At breakfast, Tish's father raised the subject of her uncle's offer.

'Back in Juba, Tish, you will do well. It is your home. Your uncle will see that you are properly cared for and when you have passed your exams you can go on to college.'

'If my uncle doesn't insist I marry,' she grimaced.

'No, daughter, he will not. He's a good man. He understands.'

Later that morning, a smart envelope bearing the crest of the boarding school fell through the letterbox. It was an offer of a free place from January. Tishala's father was delighted.

'Now, Tish, you have a choice! You can go back to your home city of Juba or take up this very good education in Britain. You are a very lucky young lady... My daughter,' he rejoiced, 'we are honoured! This is a good school!'

'I know, Daddy. But I am not like them. They are kind but I would feel different.'

'It is your choice, Tishala; I would not like to see you unhappy but the most important thing is to give you the best education; I owe it to your mother's memory.'

At lunchtime, the storm returned. The sun was hiding behind thick clouds and it began to rain. Tish fought against the wind as she climbed onto the footbridge. It was bleak and wild on the top and she clutched the rail, tightly.

Mum would not want me to be unhappy, she thought. *Dad thinks I have a choice between two options but I have three; I can stay here. I blend in here. In Bristol, all the kids have their stories – we all have a past. Black, brown, white or bright green, it doesn't matter. Bristol's like that; it's been that way for hundreds of years. I can belong here. If I work hard, I can still get good GCSEs and then, perhaps, A levels and go to college. Most of the teachers here care and if you show promise, they look after you. Let the likes of Jameson think I'm a swat, I don't care.*

As she clung to the rail, three girls from her school – each of them of a different ethnic background – approached her.

'Hi, Tish. You gonna jump or som'ing?' they laughed.

'Course not,' she smiled. 'I just like it up here.'

'You gonna leave us for that posh school, then?'

'Nah. I reckon I belong here in Bristol with me Dad... And you lot.'

'That's, like, cool! Wanna shake? We're going to the caff.'

'Like to. But I got no money.'

'No probs. It's on us. Come on.'

Christmas

Immanuel – God With Us

What comes into your mind when you think of Christmas? Christmas trees all ablaze with light, excited children ripping the paper off presents, holly berries, robins and the aroma of mince pies? Or perhaps the story of the Good News of baby Jesus come to save us. In fact, that's about the only bit of Christmas that travels – although the Australians do a good job of putting Santa on a surfboard and serving plum pudding at 40 degrees Celsius.

But I want to tell you about a Christmas I once had that was really different. It was 1970 – three years before Papua New Guinea became independent – and I was a guest at a Catholic mission station on the Sepik River.

The night before Christmas Eve resounded with the most shattering thunderstorm I have ever experienced. It was huge. The mission radio antenna was struck three times and the crashing of the thunder was all that could be heard above the noise of the torrential rain on the tin roof. The storm lasted for over an hour; water poured through cracks and ran across the floor. We measured the temperature in Fahrenheit in those days – it plummeted to 75 degrees (24 in Celsius) but the next day it was back up to its usual 90F, the humidity was as high as it could get and rivers of sweat ran of my back and chest, arms and legs.

The evening came and we set out for a church for a Christmas midnight mass further upstream along the vast and beautiful river. Our transport was a long dugout canoe beautifully managed by three sturdy men with long broad paddles. After half an hour, we pulled up at a wooden jetty and I was helped out, rubbing the blood back into my buttocks that didn't fare well in the bottom of a rocking craft designed for goods.

The priest had had his vestments carefully packed in a metal suitcase but it was not water-tight, and neither was the canoe. As the case was lifted, water poured out of it. The thin alb and chasuble were wet but at least they were clean – people were accustomed to looking bedraggled in those parts. In fact, when it rains hard, children will generally go out to play with adults not far behind them; the thing that keeps them from splashing in the river is not the water but the crocodiles.

As we followed the torch-lit path through a swamp towards the church, our feet sometimes sank up to the ankle in thick gooey mud but what bothered me most were the myriads of large fat mosquitoes that landed on my bare arms and face a dozen at a time. They made no attempt to fly away when I brushed them off with my hands – they just died in streaks of blood only to be replaced with another dozen.

Then it clouded over and began to rain again, heavily. We were all soaked to the skin – the wet vestments would no longer matter.

The church of timber, sago bark and palm was built on stilts two metres from the ground. It was accessed by a wide ladder made of long split logs. Inside, the church, full of the light of candles and electric torches, was heaving with wet, smelly bodies and more mosquitoes. The whole village was packed in, ready for the mass. We were greeted with broad smiles, revealing gleaming teeth stained pink from chewing betel nut; women fussed over us as we climbed the ladder trying not to get too much mud from the rungs on our hands. The priest was taken off to a nearby hut to vest.

The excitement increased to the sound of the beating of hand-held drums called kundus – the rhythm distinctively New Guinean – not like any Western music. A choir began the singing of carols in Pidgin – tunes recognised through layers of local cadence: *Gutpela nait, holi nait* (*Silent Night*) we sang. We were led to the front to sit on a mat reserved for us; there was a good view of the altar positioned in the centre of a large mosquito net strung from the roof. This is essential – it is not easy for a priest, his arms extended in worship, when mosquitoes settle on his face. It also guards against the occasional falling scorpion losing its footing among the thatch.

Suddenly the singing faltered. Women were shouting excitedly at the back. Everyone turned to witness a melée and panic around the west door. Men outside were calling up, '*Emi arait* – He's OK.' Apparently, the priest had fallen on the ladder. A few more scuffles and grunting followed and the priest appeared at the top of the ladder lifted by strong hands. He had been trying to climb it in his robes without getting mud on his hands and had slipped back down to the bottom. When he, at last, made his way down the aisle he was covered in light-brown goo from head to toe. His white vestments were smeared from the rungs and he even had muddy handprints up his back from the hands of his rescuers.

The priest entered the net and a bowl of clean water was brought and he washed his hands as the congregation resumed singing *Silent Night* – one of the lines describes the angels as '*nais na wait*' ('nice and white') which the priest certainly wasn't. Order, however, was restored. The mass was celebrated, people rejoiced. Immanuel, 'God with us', was a very real part of that village.

Later, I reflected on a formal mass in England at which huge care was taken with every tiny movement – the vestments were donned, each piece put on with solemn prayer, the thurible was swung at precisely the right angle in the right direction the exact number of times, each removal and replacement of the priests' birettas was done in perfect synchronicity, every bell, bow, genuflection had its own precise timing. Was Christ more or less present in that mass than amid the mud and mosquitoes? I believe Christ is wholly present wherever – there is no distinction. Christ was at home among the magi with their rich gifts but he was born in byre and laid on the straw of an animal's feeding trough.

Over the years I have experienced all kinds of worship: high and low, short and long, dramatic and solemn, loud and silent, traditional and 'fresh expression', Catholic and Protestant. Whether it be Christian Christmas, Hindu Diwali, Muslim Eid, Jewish Hanukkah, Sikh Parkash Utsav Dasveh Patshah, or a plethora of other forms, it doesn't matter that much. However we worship with our minds and actions, it is where our hearts are that counts. Immanuel will come to every open seeking heart from Planet Earth to the farthest-flung galaxy beyond our knowing; all are His and called by name.

Christmas

Christmas.
Child-charged magic;
    candy, crackers and sugar-coated,
    wide-eyed at Santa-sacks.
Yet short those years and short such delight.
The manufactured magic decays;
    merchandising mayhem is all that remains;
and Christmas dissolves in drunken haze,
    and bust-up over monopoly board or trodden-on toy trains.

That is life – bounding along the surface
keeping above the depths like a flat stone skimmed
    – each bounce shorter as the water wins –
    dreading the time when all will certainly sink.
Pretending – eyes frivolous-fixed daring not to blink.

But listen! From those dreaded depths there sounds a positive chord –
    a C-Major organ-formed with flute, diapason and pedal board.
See! There in the dense deep a firm, faint glow –
    a tiny spark in the dark –
    the Creator's mark?
Who would dare to descend and tend it?
Shall she not drown in despair long denied –
    the murk of madness where sudden dreaded drops reside?
Yet dive she must. (The tinsel and turkey no longer suffice;
    the surface froth – the fake snow and ice
    joins needle and dust when the Christmas hype dies.)

And there, where our foundation lies,
    the spark of truth is revealed — the love that comes with Christ —
God in flesh, promise-laden. Hope, joy, peace, light return!
Christ within, hearts alive, wonder-filled forever burn.

Christmas no longer needs magic when truth and heavenly highs
Transcend even love-baked pudding and delicious mince pies!

Contact

Bob was not as young as he once was. Whenever he travelled alone – something he often did – he would find himself sitting, perhaps for hours, next to someone he would never meet in any other context. He rarely went to parties, and those he did grace were to meet people with similar interests – as were the conferences he attended but the older Bob became, the more he found people would share all sorts of things with him.

Bob is an author and thus of interest – also someone with a website which could be downloaded and his identity verified. It helps that Bob likes people and rarely finds them boring or dull.

Thus on this occasion, involving a bus, a train, two planes and two more buses, Bob met a heave of sixth formers, a woman with twin babies a few months old (on a seven-hour flight – interesting!), and a man anxious to tell him he was only on the plane because he got his seat with an offer a quarter of the price. (You should never want to know what the next guy paid!). On discovering Bob had worked in Africa as a Church volunteer, he declared, 'My God, you don't believe in that God nonsense do you?!' All this, Bob found fascinating.

It was, however, a young student that engaged him the most. Maisie was not yet twenty-one and was in the middle of an English degree course at an American university. The story began when she was forced to turn off her devices for take-off. Her first year had gone reasonably well, she told him but the second year was proving more difficult. She was just finishing a trip home for Christmas, which hadn't helped. Her boyfriend from her teenage years had discovered some new exciting interest in her absence and had taken the opportunity to dump her on Christmas Eve. It wasn't the end of the world – she was never that keen on him – but it was the pain of being dumped by someone you thought was a reliable friend on the very night that was supposed to be full of promise.

'This year Christmas has been, like, yuk,' said Maisie half to herself. 'I'm glad to get away – even if the course is beginning to suck.'

Bob listened. He supplied tissues. All the other passengers were back in their own worlds glued to screens with earphones inserted. Maisie apologised and became embarrassed. Bob told her it was a long time since he was at

university – and he was not finding her tale boring or embarrassing, and certainly not an imposition; Maisie was interesting.

'Why isn't your second year so good?' Bob asked.

Her tutor, it turned out, was a nihilist (or claimed to be – his lifestyle, Maisie thought, was at odds with his intellectual philosophy).

'Anything that I wrote last term that, like, implied the world was a teeny bit positive, he called a "human construct",' she explained. She had been forced to back up everything she said and, as an undergraduate, she lacked the knowledge to do that easily, while with decades of study behind him her tutor demolished her every step. He insisted that anything she described as good news was, in fact, an illusion.

'I didn't believe him but I couldn't think of anything that he didn't rubbish. He said Christmas was a load of crap – only he used posh words to say it … And, now, this Christmas has turned out to be mostly that.'

Inside, Bob was cross. This girl had been badly treated – both at university (tutors should never make their students feel like rubbish) and at home. He wanted to tell her that the world was full of good news – packed full of love, and joy was real, and so were the Christmas legends – not the tales themselves, necessarily but the truths that lay behind them; Bob had encountered that Light in a dark world. Yet he was patient – Maisie needed to find some of that Light for herself.

'It can't be *all* bad. Aren't there any good things about your university?' he asked.

Maisie's list was quite long – her fellow students, the great literature she had uncovered, the lecturers she liked, and the campus was beautiful.

'Are all these people and things, "human constructs"?' Bob asked.

'Of course not,' she replied. *Where was he going with this?*

'What were the best bits about Christmas when you were a child – the bits you can remember?'

Maisie didn't mind answering, 'The lights, the tree, the smells, the presents, the carols, I suppose … Uncle Tom reading to me … and that year we built a snowman with him – with Uncle Tom … and lots of other things.'

'Are the tree and the smells and presents and stuff still the same?' asked Bob.

'Yes, but Uncle Tom wasn't there this year – he's too old to travel.'

'So,' said Bob, 'Uncle Tom was, and still is, real – not made up? His love is genuine and not a human construct.'

Maisie laughed. 'I wondered where you were going with this. You're clever … I want you to come to one of my tutorials,' she declared.

'No,' Bob assured her, 'you don't need me – you know for yourself that love is real. Just remember that. Let your tutor have his rant. Keep it real in your heart. Have you called Uncle Tom and told him you missed him? He's probably missed you as much as you missed him.'

'Yeah, true. I'll call him as soon as I get off this plane... Who are you?' Maisie quizzed, astonished at how her travelling companion had turned her day on its head, 'An angel?'

'Oh, me? I write books.'

'What sort of books?'

'Books that talk about hope and joy and love in a dark world.'

Maisie did not turn on her devices again that day. When she got back to her digs she downloaded some of Bob's stories onto her phone and looked up John, chapter 1. Her tutor believed, of course, that Christianity was a human construct but somehow, that night, Maisie knew she was loved. Whatever her tutor said, she believed in angels. She'd met one. What was it that Bob had said? 'Keep it real in your heart.'

True Wisdom

A reflection of a Magus

So what's in a star you might ask? Well I mean, apart from it being millions of miles away on the roof of the cosmos. To be honest, there is so much we don't know about the stars; that's why it's important to study them. It was only a few years ago that everyone believed the world was a flat disk standing on enormous pillars – some, even, that it was borne up by giant elephants! That, I must confess, was rather fanciful. What were the poor creatures going to have to eat? Everyone knows that living creatures need food to survive.

Plenty of people still believe the world is flat, though. Not us wise men. We have read the scientific explanations and studied the maths. Have you noticed that you can only see so far across the sea? It's called the horizon. If you climb a tall cliff, however, you can see further. It's because the world is a sphere – not flat. That's been studied carefully and some wise men have done their sums and worked out how big our world is. And all around the ball, we call Earth, there is a roof of stars. They move together – most of them are fixed. Some like the sun and the moon and the wanderers – the planets – obey different laws but they remain ordered. If you do the maths you can predict which stars will rise and when; to the wise, the heavens are a foreseeable sphere. Yet sometimes, rarely, there is one that is different – one that can't be foretold.

A month ago there was a new star – really bright and beautiful. I and my wise friends watched it carefully for a whole week. It always set in the same place over the western horizon in the direction of Judaea on the other side of the desert. People were asking us what it all meant. They would, of course, because we are magi and it's our job to interpret the meaning of things – especially stars. We might have much to learn but you can still tell a lot from the stars – the ordinary ones tell us about ordinary life but this star was so special – new and bright; it must mean something really wonderful.

Now the wise thing to do is not just guess or make something up. After all, we are scientists, so we studied the ancient Hebrew writings from Judaea. There is nothing about a star in their writings – they are about their relationship with their God – but there is plenty about expecting a new king to be born as a baby. There was only one choice for wise men with a scientific background to make – go and look. But if we were going to come upon a new king, then he was bound to be greater than any other – only someone really special can have such a magnificent star just for them! We arranged presents, then, fit for such a king. Gold, frankincense – the best our land could offer – and the finest myrrh. A wise man cannot be a mean one.

It's at this point I have to be honest with you. For time immemorial the custom is to give all the credit for wise decisions to men – I mean *men* as opposed to *women*. The thing is, whether you like it or not, people scoff at the idea that women can be wise. That is rubbish. A wise man is one who listens to the wise words of the women in his life. Half the wisdom in the world comes from women – it's just that the men get the credit. In years to come, if this star really means there is a new baby king, then people might talk about our visit – the visit of the wise men – but, believe me, if we hadn't have been wise enough to take our wives with us we would not be remembered at all. Well, certainly not as wise. I will go as far as to say that the wisest thing a wise man can do is listen to the wise words of his wife – and the wisest thing a wise woman can do is listen to the wise words of her husband. Do the maths – two wise heads are going to be three times wiser than one single wise one. That's because, when it is shared, wisdom grows to, at least, half as much again. On their own, no matter how wise, a person can make so many mistakes that people doubt their wisdom. So with three wise men and three wise women, you can calculate just how much wisdom we had between us – you do the maths!

So the six of us packed our camels and set off. We could have gone the long way round – the usual way, north via the rivers – but we had good camels and knew the stars so we headed off into the desert towards Ammon – which the Greeks renamed Philadelphia. Don't get me wrong – even this shortcut is five hundred miles and it's desert all the way except for a few oases, so you have to get things right. It took us almost a month. Finally, we crossed the River Jordan and put up in Jericho. After that the desert road to Jerusalem and on to the palace. Well, where else would you expect to find a baby destined to be king?

The old king is Herod. They call him 'the great'; if you look at the things he has built and the size of his army, you can see why. He's not a nice chap, though; he has the reputation of a tyrant and so it proved.

Seeing as we looked sufficiently distinguished, he granted us an audience. He summoned his own wise men, too – scholars who knew their scriptures. They put us on to a verse that suggested the baby would be born in Bethlehem – a village seven miles to the south. You could see Herod was kind of jealous but he put a smile on his face and told us that if we found the child, to return and let him know, so he could visit and worship him also. That sounded awfully suspicious but we thanked him and followed the directions he gave to the village.

The star was now right overhead; we were clearly in the right place. We asked around in the village and everyone knew who we were talking about. Shepherds had seen a choir of angels and had been guided to the stable of an inn. The baby had been born there because there was no room for them inside. They had put the baby in a manger but the innkeeper had quickly made room for them the next day. The locals called the baby 'Joshua', which is Hebrew for 'Jesus', after a legendary hero who had saved his people.

It was then that we really started to feel, well, kind of out of place. This was a very strange place for a new king but it was right – the star proved it. It was then that the wise women took over.

'Look fellas,' declared my wife, wisely. 'This kid is in an ordinary – less than ordinary – place but they all know he's special. Shepherds might not be noted for their wisdom but they can recognise a choir of angels like anyone else. Apparently, they've even presented him with a lamb. That's generous but what are they going to do with a live lamb? And, come to that, what are they going to do with a gold bar, frankincense and myrrh? I ask you, fellas, what does a new baby need if his parents are rock bottom poor?'

'A pile of nappies,' declared one of the other wise wives.

'Absolutely,' agreed the third. 'And several changes of swaddling clothes.'

They had us all traipse back to Jerusalem and visit the souk. I must say they have everything in that place – it's quite a tourist spot. We didn't seem to stand out there at all. Before long we had added nappies, swaddling clothes, towels, soap and sweet-smelling baby powder, and even a couple of changes of clothes for the mother to add to our presents.

Back in Bethlehem, we knocked gently on the door. Mary and Joseph were receiving all sorts of guests as the news had got around and they were pleased but not really amazed to see us from the East. They said that the new baby was directly from God and that if he was to be a king, he would be the king of everywhere on Earth. They accepted our rich presents graciously – they were a sign that even Gentiles – which means foreigners – appreciated his worth but it was the practical gifts that brought smiles and joy – Mary (for that was the mother's name) said that the nappies and clothes were an answer to prayer. Her husband, Joseph, had never doubted that God would ensure they would have all they needed but to see their need met with the wisdom of three wise women warmed their hearts. Somehow women can see things we men miss, and vice versa – none of the women had noticed the star in the first place, for example. It goes to prove that the wisest people are those who do things as a team.

King Herod should have learnt that. We all had the same dream that night: it warned us not to go back to Jerusalem because that monster would have had baby Jesus killed. The terrible thing is that after we had been home for a couple of months we got word that Herod had ordered the killing of all the babies in Bethlehem but, by that time, Mary, Joseph and Jesus had left. Some say they went to Egypt.

All that was several years ago now. We've never seen a star like that since. Herod, the so-called great, died just two years after Jesus was born and we have always wondered what had happened to the baby but last week we got a message from his parents. They were safe – all of them – and Jesus was doing well. They are now living in Nazareth where Joseph has a carpenter's shop. They just wanted us to know that our gifts had come in really handy while they were refugees in Egypt.

We've carried on trying to be wise, of course, but somehow searching out baby Jesus will always stand out as the wisest thing we ever did. We look forward to him coming into his kingdom; the world certainly needs him.

God and Creation

Winter Sunrise

Mist-shrouded dawn, striae of cloud, sun's rays scattering,
Glory-streaked in purples, orange, and pale blue hues.
While bush-perched robin sings, his song lost amidst clattering
dust cart and chattering children's school-bound shoes.

Old folk at bedroom window wake, watch, wonder ... and weep,
As a wild mother utters shrill obscenities, kids shriek
And dogs' barks rend the air, waking the hedgehog in the compost heap.
But the robin, oblivious to all, sings on as the daybreak din reaches its peak.

Van doors bang, engines roar, exhaust pipes belch noxious oxides;
Young eyes water, tiny throats sting as the choking haze, child-height, swirls ...
Yet amongst the spoils of polluted air, God's creations' power resides:
Daffodils reach up, topped with pregnant buds, camellia's pink corolla unfurls,

The robin still sings shrill, the hedgehog dodges the snuffling dog,
And shafts of winter sun stretch, dispelling the last lingering wisps of fog.

Unconditional Love

There was once a young man who set out on a journey to explore the world. He took with him a rucksack containing the essential things he would need on the way – a tent, a little food, bedding and spare clothes.

He hadn't gone far before he came across a sow who had just given birth to piglets. She had no shelter and it was threatening rain.

'I will care for you,' he said and he traded some clothes for enough wood, borrowed some tools from a cottager and built the sow a sty. The pig gave a contented grunt as her piglets crowded in with her.

The following day the young man rose early. He had just enough food left for breakfast but then he must find work to earn a little to assist him on his journey. It wasn't long before he came across a homeless man with an empty bottle beside him. The strong smell of alcohol barely disguised the fetid stench of the man's emaciated body. On seeing the young man, the beggar raised his bottle and demanded the young man give him something to eat or drink. People were walking by, most making sure they looked the other way but the young man gave him his last breakfast and said, 'Do not worry, I will care for you.'

A hundred metres down the road he called into an inn and asked if he could work his lodging and board for a few days. The landlord was only too pleased to hire a fit young man for the cost of a meal or two and at the end of each day gave him a small silver coin as a wage which the traveller passed to the man without a home.

Yet after three days the man was even more decrepit than the first time he had seen him and he realised that without proper care the man would die, so he asked the landlord if he could work double-time and give the man without a home a bed. He did this until the man was strong again and then left him to work at the inn. But a day later the man became drunk and found himself back on the streets.

So the young man came back and gave him his tent and bedding and got him treatment for his addiction.

'Why do you do this for a man who devours all you do for him?' asked the landlord.

'Because his addiction does not define him,' replied the young man. 'It may be this day he will overcome it.'

Five years later, the young man came by again and found the man without a home unconscious in the road where he had been left to die, so the young man took him to hospital and paid for his treatment. 'Maybe this time,' he said. 'His addiction does not define him.'

And that, my friends, is just what God does for us, his rebellious people. He does it in the hope that someday some of us will recognise him and respond with love. He does it because some people do – if only for a day. He does it because he loves and cannot turn his back on us. Our sinful nature does not define us; we are created in unconditional love, to love unconditionally.

The Creator

The following began life as a reflection on creation in Winds and Wonders from The White Gates series before I added to it for inclusion in *Adventures with God.* I offer it again here.

At the beginning, all was formless and empty, and the dark was deep.

Then the Creator spoke.

Her Spirit, her Breath, her powerful Winds fell upon the chaos.

There was an explosion of new order.

The laws of nature came into being, dimension upon dimension.

Light illuminated the darkness.

Life and love followed.

All was wonderful beyond measure.

Again, She created.

She begot a race of people with bodies, minds and hearts designed

to explore, discern, feel and love all that She had called into being.

And, then, She, who is all-love,

touched the people she had made –

she fired them, inspired them with her Winds,

so that they, too, grew, knew and spoke.

Even before the beginning

She had chosen each of them to become holy and pure.

She loved them beyond all measure –

loved them even before they were created.

She poured into them the power to love as she loves.

But the people she had made abused that power and rejected her.

Yet her love was undimmed and through that love
She gave of her very Self.
The Creator emptied herself of her God-power
and became one of them in time, for a time,
to restore and give new birth to all that she had made.
She absorbed every anger, heat, hate and blame
and turned it into love and flawless life.

Then, at the last,
She bequeathed them her Breath again
to lead them to love again –
the firstfruits of an eternal New Creation,
full of the Winds and Wonders of God.

Jairus' Daughter

It's quite hot – the sun is strong. There is a whiff of fish in the air. Jesus and his disciples sail up to the jetty on the lakeside. This is the Lake of Galilee. It's a huge lake, so big, some call it a 'sea' - but you can see the other side. Jesus has been on a preaching tour there and is just coming back.

There is a huge, noisy crowd. All sorts of people are crowding around wanting to listen to Jesus' teaching. He's outside of Jairus'? house. Jesus went inside an hour ago and has just come out. Let's hear what Joseph, the servant of Jairus, has to tell us.

Hi. I'm Joseph. Let me tell you what Jesus has just done. I was there all through it.

As soon as word went out that Jesus'? boat was coming our way, many people headed down to the shore. There were many who were sick – the walking sick, and relatives of those who weren't. Jesus is quite famous for healing people – although, mostly, he teaches about God. Some say he only does his miracles to illustrate a point but if you're desperate, it doesn't stop you from hoping. We were desperate – we who lived at Jairus' house that is.

You see, little Ruth... I say '?little' but she's growing up fast – she's twelve, almost grown-up some would say. Though to us who have known her all her life she's still our little girl but last night she was taken really ill. It was sudden. Some sort of fever – and that's scary because when a person's temperature goes up like that – well, they could die. And she is only twelve – not that old to resist a powerful fever. What caused it we don't know. None of the rest of the house got sick. It may have been something to do with the bad air we get this time of year – but, anyway, that's beside the point. She was really sick. The doctor was hopeless – and Jairus himself is the ruler of the synagogue, and he was doing all the praying he could. He even paid a group of women to pray – but what good the prayers of people are who only do it for money, I don't know. But then, we heard Jesus was on his way. Could this be an answer to our prayers – the genuine ones that is?

So Jairus strode down to the lakeside to meet Jesus as soon as he stepped ashore. He took me along with him. As he's the ruler of the synagogue, the crowd parted to allow him through. Most thought that he had come to formally welcome Jesus – which was a good thing because so often the religious authorities didn't like him. It doesn'?t help when more people turn out to listen to Jesus than ever turn up to the synagogue on the Sabbath – the thing is, you can't compete with feeding thousands of people. I mean thousands – 5000 on one occasion and 4000 on another. But I knew why Jairus had come out. He was desperate, just like the others hoping for a miracle.

Sometimes I feel sorry for Jesus. He'?d just come across the lake but instead of getting a chance to sit down for a drink and freshen up in one of the lakeside taverns, he'd got pulled every which way by the crowd but he coped with it brilliantly. As I said, he doesn't heal everybody – when he does he always makes a point about God and the bigger picture – a picture that isn't just for now but forever. That'?s why people like to listen to him – he is quite certain that God includes everyone – even servants like me and my family.

Well, I wasn't expecting him to accept Jairus' invitation to come to his house to do a miracle for Ruth but he did. It might have been because she was a kid – I don't know. He loves children and always blesses them when their mums bring them to him. So he commanded – he always speaks with authority – he commanded Jairus to take him to his house.

The rest of the crowd didn't give up, though. The noise – well you could hardly hear yourself think – and the smell. Some of these people had come straight from the fish market. There was a particular woman; I didn't notice her among the others. She must have just managed to reach through and touch Jesus' clothes. Jesus just stood still and turned round. He held up his hand and everybody stopped calling out.

To cut a long story short, she had been healed. I can tell you about it later if you want but just then I was frustrated. Jairus was too. You see, we hoped that Jesus would come straight to Ruth. I knew she could die any time but now, here Jesus was, stopping off to cure people who weren't going to die that moment. That woman had been going to the doctors for twelve years, from almost before Ruth was born! She was not an emergency. How many more was Jesus going to heal on the way?

Then came devastating news. My fellow servant came running down the street. He took Jairus' sleeve. He was out of breath and upset.

'Master, I... I have to tell you that Ruth... that Ruth has... has... has gone... She went very peacefully...'?

I was stunned. I know I am only a servant but I loved that little girl. Jairus just wept. Jesus turned away from the woman and looked at him. Jairus said, 'It's too late master, she's died... You stay on here – these people need you.'

Jesus looked at him. I mean, really looked at him, in the eyes. It was like looking at love, powerful love. And then he said: 'Don'?t be afraid, only believe... Take me to her.'

We walked quickly to the house. The women brought in to pray, were letting out the terrible cry that you only get from professional wailers.

'Shut up and get out,' commanded Jesus, 'the girl is not dead, only sleeping.'

The women turned off their wailing. They did leave but not before they laughed in his face. They had seen enough dead people to know that Ruth was definitely dead. I saw her too. Her body was... empty. It didn't really look like her at all. I had *heard* that Jesus had brought people back to life but had dismissed it. This wasn't Jesus' usual style...?

Anyway, now you could hear a pin drop. What was Jesus going to do? Everyone was looking at him. He just went up to the bed, and said quietly: 'Hello, little girl.' And he took her hand... picked up her dead hand and held it, just held it gently... And then, in a strong, powerful commanding voice – I shall never forget it – he called out: '*Talitha Koum!* Little girl, rise up!', and he, kind of, pulled her up. She sat on the edge of the bed, and then Jesus pulled again, tugging her onto her feet. Ruth just stood there, looking at everyone – Jesus wasn't holding her anymore – he was holding her mother instead because she was about to faint. We were all shocked. Everyone just gasped. And then Jesus said, gently to her mother. 'I think she would like something to eat. I guess she'll be pretty hungry... Is that right, Ruth?'

Ruth nodded. 'Yeah. I'm starving,'? just like she always said when she got in from her lessons.

Her father looked at me, and I knew what to do. I rushed down to the kitchen. There was no one there but our cook soon followed me. All we could find was some fresh bread and honey. Cook said she would work on Ruth's favourite food right away.

Well, it was amazing just how Ruth tucked into the bread and honey. She was sitting down with Jesus and asking her parents what all the fuss was about. She hadn't been aware of just how sick she had been. They told her that Jesus had given her a special blessing, and they were all so honoured.

'Yeah. Thanks Jesus,' she said. 'That's cool... After Jesus has gone, can I go round and see my friend Esther and tell her about it?'

'Of course but I think the master might like to stay and rest a bit...'

'No, it's time for me to go," said Jesus. 'I want to tell this crowd a story, and then send them home. I'm going to stay at Simon Peter's place tonight. You have a lovely daughter, Jairus. Mind you look after her well.'

'Thank you master. I certainly will. Will you bless us all before you leave?' So Jesus did.

Now you see him here, teaching. He never stops, this Jesus. If you want my opinion, he is straight from God. I don't care what the teachers of the law say.

Harvest Song

Gathering in. August sun warm in sweet-scented lanes.
Reaping rich, ripe, abundant, garnered grains,
Sung home, sung in with lively lays and lusty strains.
Harvest home. Barns full and tight, against winter rains.

January field, brown and empty. Stripped of weed.
Tilled and drilled. The song is sung to pipe and reed.
Winter wheat, barley for beer, maize for feed.
Blue-flowering flax, hardy oat and yellow rapeseed.

April shoots lengthen green and bright,
A new song of joy strikes up at the sight.
Dibbing for spuds, potting beans for frost's flight
June, July rejoicing, songs of summer's height.

Yet, harvest is the heartiest, unfettered merriest sway.
Birdsong mingled with cries of lovers bouncing in the hay.
Harvest home! Here's time to sing as September sun's last ray
Writes the notes, thrills the heart, pens the way.

Yet there is deepness here beyond the field. For all year long
Glimpses of hope and life in a world of pain and wrong.
Here, promise of bliss and beauty join in eternal soul-throng.
To God we belong, to him we return when heaven is filled with harvest song.

But now, today, we live and love, bound and belonging to Earth,
Formed from stardust, ever new and of infinite worth,
Forgiven. blessed. precious and treasured by our boundless Creator.

Dear Reader, Listen. Give. Grow. Become. For you are no mere spectator!

ACKNOWLEDGEMENTS

I am truly indebted to everyone who has inspired, advised and encouraged me in writing these pages. They come from working with a great variety of people over many decades in different countries and communities.

Over the last few months, a few people have given me direct help. Emily Owen, Mary Cookson and Pip Lovell, and, of course, my wife, Tina, have all done sterling work at various points during the compiling of this anthology.

I am am absolutely delighted to have worked alongside Anna Hewett-Rakthanee. I hope and pray that she will have many more opportunities to bring her talent to the world in the years to come.

I give all the proceeds of my books to charity. My default charity is Confident Children out of Conflict in Juba, South Sudan, so I thank you for your purchase and contributions. This organisation not only rescues children - mainly girls - from the streets, taking them into a place of love and safety but also sees that they get proper nutrition and education.

Last but not least I give thanks to God who has taken me from unpromising beginnings to a place of fulfilment, hope and joy. My prayer is that many more will find that same light in their lives.

'For it is the God who said, "Let light shine out of darkness," who has shone in our hearts to give the light of the knowledge of the glory of God in the face of Jesus Christ.' 2 Corinthians 4:6

Trevor Stubbs
November 2021

Lightning Source UK Ltd.
Milton Keynes UK
UKHW032043090822
407057UK00005B/142

9 781915 288004